THE
RESURRECTIONIST

THE
RESURRECTIONIST

GARY K. WOLF

DOUBLEDAY & COMPANY, INC.
GARDEN CITY, NEW YORK

1979

All of the characters in this book
are fictitious, and any resemblance
to actual persons, living or dead,
is purely coincidental.

ISBN: 0-385-13141-0
Library of Congress Catalog Card Number 77–12894

*My grateful thanks to Ed Lee, President,
Pro-Log Corporation, for his technical
advice and his good humor.*

ACKNOWLEDGMENT

Parts of Chapter 22 appeared in somewhat different form in the story "The Bridge Builder" in *Orbit 14*, copyright 1974 by Damon Knight.

THE
RESURRECTIONIST

CHAPTER 1

A no-nonsense vision of competence in her crisply starched silver and blue Bridge Authority uniform, the transportal hostess entered the terminal's Luminary Lounge.

"Time to depart," she told her celebrity charge in flawless Russian. She handed her ward a foil-encased capsule and a crystal goblet filled with water.

Galina Rosmanov snubbed her harsh American cigarillo into the marble ashtray beside her, stood, and carefully smoothed the wrinkles out of her decidedly nonsocialistic tailored wool suit, cashmere sweater and unborn-calf-skin coat. As a sop to Russia's current campaign to have its prominent citizens dress in peasant clothing to foster greater association with the general populace, she knotted a babushka around her head. It was pure silk. She had paid a hundred dollars for it in an exclusive boutique on San Francisco's Union Square.

Galina accepted the capsule, ripped it free of its foil enclosure, and swallowed it with a hasty gulp of water. Without the capsule, recovery time following a trip through the wires lasted a flat twenty-four hours regardless of the journey's length. The capsule, mainly a hybrid synthesis of stimulants and vasodilators, reduced this recovery time to sixty minutes.

Galina walked out of the lounge and into the corridor leading to the transportals. A flock of reporters, pleading for tidbits of gossip the way insatiable hordes of pigeons beg for peanuts in the park, immediately engulfed her.

"Miss Rosmanov. Is it true you're planning to request political asylum in . . ."

"Harry Kile. 'CBS Evening News.' Here in Mexico City with

Galina Rosmanov, world-famous dancer with the Kirov Ballet. Tell us, Galina . . ."

"Hey, honey. Let's have a pretty smile. Come on, a big dazzler. Pretty girl like you ought to show what you've got. Come on now. You can do better than . . ."

"Galina, you've been linked romantically with a number of leading political figures. Could you tell me, as one woman to another, which one was the best . . ."

Her tiny heels clicked on the stone floor as Galina quickened her pace, leaving the reporters behind. She ducked through a plate-glass door, which her hostess held open for her, one of six doors marked "Washington Predeparture." Her hostess entered after her, shut the door behind them, and locked it leaving the reporters shoving helplessly against it as if they were goldfish attempting to penetrate through their bowl to the illusion of infinite freedom beyond.

The transportal, a ten-foot-square, smoked-glass and chrome, cathedral-domed structure occupied the far third of the room. A traveler had just stepped inside. A blue haze filled the transportal, cleared, and the traveler was gone, on his way through the wires to Washington.

Galina's hostess began her canned predeparture recitation. To her credit, it came out sounding totally spontaneous. But then it should have. The Bridge Authority had spent a great deal of money training her to say things she did not understand to people she did not care about.

"You'll experience a slight tingle, nothing unpleasant, a hot flash, and you'll be there. You'll feel slightly woozy on the other end. Don't worry, it's a perfectly normal sensation. There will be a hostess standing by to make sure you don't accidently stumble and fall. You'll rest in our Luminary Lounge for an hour, undergo a simple medical check to insure your complete recovery, and you'll be on your way." Mentally the hostess ran through her checklist to see if she had forgotten anything. As usual, she hadn't. She was one of the best hostesses in the system, consistently awarded the Bridge Authority's Efficiency and Encouragement Pin, bestowed for adhering strictly to procedures while displaying the widest possible smile. "Can I answer any questions?"

Galina shook her head.

"Just to double-check, have you had any alcoholic beverages or tranquilizers within the past hour?" Depressants countered the effect of the capsule and tended to lengthen recovery time. Abstaining from them was the procedure celebrities most often ignored.

Again the headshake.

"Good. And you have taken your pill? No fudging?" Amazing how many people feared the capsule more than the wires.

Galina nodded.

"Fine. Passport and visa? One last check."

Galina fished them from her Gucci bag and displayed them. A red, white, and blue border framed the plastic visa. The passport bore a hammer and sickle and, inside, a terribly grainy photograph. It was so full of entry stamps, the U.S. authorities would probably have to bind in a supplemental page in order to emblazon it with their intricate flying eagle.

"Super. As soon as you're fully recovered, you'll be processed immediately through immigration. I've already alerted them, so your inconvenience should be minimal." A red light winked on above their heads. "That means they're ready for you at weigh-in. Before you go, I'd like to say that it's been my pleasure assisting you, and on behalf of myself and the entire Bridge Authority, I wish you a swift and pleasant journey." The hostess cracked an honestly sincere smile. After this traveler, she would go off shift and could begin preparing for her heavy date in Toronto that evening.

Galina moved into the weigh-in room. Her luggage, a beige and red striped Gucci suitcase that matched her bag, and an olive-drab steamer trunk, awaited her, ferried there by conveyor. Galina stepped onto a large electronic scale. The transfer technician entered her weight, 43 kilos, into his program. Her suitcase weighed 16 kilos, her trunk 22. He factored this data into the program, too. Then he carefully double-checked his measurements. Matter transference greatly resembled a game of billiards, the trick being to give travelers just enough momentum to reach their destination. Get them going too fast and they might overshoot, too slow and they might stall in the wires. Initial thrust hinged directly upon

weight, hence weigh-in required extreme precision. An error of as little as one half of a per cent could prove fatal.

Satisfied that his readings were accurate, the technician directed Galina into a glassed-in isolation cubicle, one of three leading directly to the transportal. Her luggage rolled inside with her atop the conveyor belt. The traveler immediately ahead of Galina was inside the transportal ready to leave. The familiar blue haze filled the structure, and the traveler disappeared.

Matter transmitted through wires had a tendency to spread out over distance. Hence very few travelers went directly to their destinations. Most were shunted through a complex web of collector stations where their disassembled bodies were reconsolidated. There were twelve of these stations between Mexico City and Washington, and they accounted for a full three minutes of the trip's five-minute duration.

The technician's arrival light winked on, signifying the previous traveler's safe arrival in Washington.

The technician thumbed the switch that opened the glass door giving Galina access to the transportal. She stepped inside. Her luggage slipped off the conveyor belt into a bin beside her.

"The weather in Washington today is cold and sunny, highs expected around zero, lows tonight dipping to below minus ten," the technician said brightly as he made his final adjustments. "I hope you have your long underwear with you." He flipped the switch sending Galina Rosmanov on her way.

The sending light blinked off.

But the arrival light stayed dim. Five, six, seven minutes. Far too long. Something had gone wrong. Suddenly, every malfunction indicator on the technician's control panel flashed on simultaneously in the electronic equivalent of a distress cry.

The technician pushed the standby button with one hand, the alarm button with the other.

Within moments, Ralph Ferguson, Bridge Authority safety director, was on the phone from Bridge Authority headquarters in Washington, D.C.

"Sir," gulped the technician, "I'm afraid we have a Code One here in Mexico City."

In the matter transference business, problems didn't come any worse.

CHAPTER 2

Half an hour later Saul Lukas arrived in Mexico City. The Bridge Authority paid Saul a million-dollar-a-year retainer. In return he provided them with a rather difficult-to-explain service. He wasn't an engineer; he would have been hard pressed to describe the workings of a bridge in any but the simplest of terms. His lack of a college or even a high school degree disqualified him for a managerial or even a managerial training post. His fierce individualism and reluctance to follow orders made him an unlikely candidate for a blue-collar position.

But Saul had something the Bridge Authority valued far more than an M.B.A., double-E, or trade school degree. Saul had a penetrating, hard-nosed, effective approach to problem solving, and the problems the Bridge Authority tossed his way were the biggest the company had.

According to well-guarded Bridge Authority statistics, travelers could be expected to foul up inside the wires once in every 10,850,000 transfers. Saul's corporate function: get these travelers out. Alive.

The Bridge Authority carried Saul near the apex of their pyramidal organizational chart, inside a block labeled Safety Consultant. But corporate executives referred to him instead as the Resurrectionist, the man who dragged the living dead back from electrical purgatory.

He answered only to Michelle Warren, Bridge Authority president. It had been Michelle, with her belief in the need for prioritization, who had instituted the practice of rating missing travelers one through four according to their jobs, the size of their families, their hometowns, and especially their prominence and the prominence of their relatives.

Codes 2, 3, and 4 encompassed college students heading home for the holidays, grandmothers off to visit their heirs, salesmen leaving on business trips. The people who would stay page-one news only for a day or two, then fade unnoticed into oblivion. Code 1 designated a celebrity. A potential international incident. A *Time* cover story crying for more research into the technique of matter transference. A congressional investigating committee delving into Bridge Authority safety controls.

Saul openly scoffed at her codes, paying them no attention whatsoever. Wires equalized everything, everybody. Inside those finger-thick copper and gold highways, social standing, influence, wealth held no significance whatsoever. The only thing that mattered to anyone caught inside was the uncategorizable talent of Saul Lukas, a thirty-six-year-old uneducated excop from Cincinnati. Himself a Code 4 straight down the line.

Riding wire always sent an adult's temperature up three or four degrees, so Saul awoke in the Luminary Lounge with a slight flush. He shook his tall, slender frame to work the stiffness out of his joints. He felt totally refreshed and slightly euphoric, as travelers always did after a trip through the wires. The sensation was partly a residual effect of the capsule, partly a real physical regeneration. Early fears that transference would cause harmful disruptions to the body's metabolism had totally failed to prove out. Instead, the opposite had occurred. Inflamed tissue did not rematerialize as readily as healthy tissue. Riding wire wouldn't cure cancer, but for razor burns, acne, and hemorrhoids, it was the greatest cure-all since Lourdes.

Ralph Ferguson was already conferring with several engineers and technicians in the recovery lounge when Saul came around. "Saul. Good to see you again." He extended his hand with the reluctance of a man forced to paw through a garbage sack in search of a missing salad fork.

"How you been, Ralph?" Saul rubbed his forehead, his hand's shadow bringing into high relief the diagonal scar above his eye, and the twisted nose that hinted at more than one encounter with a fist.

Taking Ralph's hand for support, Saul slipped off his bed and, with Ralph beside him, headed toward the transportal lounges clustered, as in all Bridge Authority terminals, around the circular building's central power hub.

"Who is it?" Saul asked.

"Galina Rosmanov." Ralph assumed the woman's name alone would immediately identify her to anyone, even Saul.

But Saul and Ralph traveled in opposite circles, opera houses and polo fields versus pool halls and basketball courts. "So who's she?"

"Galina Rosmanov? The ballerina? With the Russians' Kirov Ballet?"

Saul shook his head. The only dancers he ever watched performed topless and wore G-strings. "Where was she headed?"

"She danced last night at the Palace of Fine Arts here in Mexico City. She was on her way to Washington, D.C. She was to have danced *Romeo and Juliet* with Alexei Drashow at the Kennedy Center this weekend. I had tickets for it myself." Ralph had paid a scalper nearly $400 for the pair and had bragged about it for weeks to his chums. Since the lot of them measured culture in terms of its cost, they considered him a very discriminating figure indeed.

"What was she carrying?"

"Two pieces. A suitcase and a steamer trunk." Ralph handed Saul a computer printout listing three weights. Since the technology of matter transference dealt with pure volume only, the printout didn't differentiate between Galina Rosmanov and her luggage. Saul found this attitude typical of the Bridge Authority as a whole.

"What about Michelle?" Saul asked.

"She'll be here in an hour or so. She had a few corporate loose ends to tie down."

"She always does." Saul spoke from experience. Michelle was his exwife.

Saul and Ralph entered the departure section. Swarms of newsmen, many of whom had followed Galina Rosmanov down the same corridor not two hours earlier, converged on them, besieging them with questions. Ralph slickly droned out a few nonspecifics.

Situation under control. Minor malfunction. Have her out in no time. Nothing to worry about. Saul, more concerned with practicalities than public relations, knew better, but said nothing.

Bridge Authority guards cordoned off the hallway leading to the doors marked "Washington Predeparture," permitting only ticket-holding passengers inside. Ralph and Saul entered the middle door, the same one Galina Rosmanov had taken. The transportal glowed a reddish orange signifying it had been placed on active shutdown. Like everything else in the wire network, it had a backup so service could continue without interruption. The backup transportal stood on the other side of a smoked Plexiglas divider. There weren't many travelers going out on it though, probably less than half the normal number. Traffic always dropped off radically on a line after an accident. Word got around. Like screams from inside the dentist's office. Nobody wanted to be next.

The technician who had been on duty when Galina Rosmanov disappeared, sat off to one side, his head cupped in his hands. A lawyer, provided him by his labor union, stood beside him, resting a hand soothingly on his shoulder. A bulge under the lawyer's arm betrayed the presence of a voice-actuated pocket recorder able to capture every conversation within a ten-foot radius.

"What happened?" Saul asked the technician.

"I have instructed my client to answer no questions pending board review," the lawyer answered. The Federal Transportation Agency, the government regulatory body overseeing operation of the Bridge Authority, would convene a board to ascertain the cause of the incident. Conceivably, if the technician were found to be at fault, he could be held on charges ranging from criminal negligence to manslaughter. "Until then, we have nothing to say." The lawyer set his jaw and squared his shoulders. Flash frozen and cut off at the chest he would have replicated any of a thousand busts on display in any of a thousand law school corridors.

"There's a woman's life at stake here," Saul reminded him. "While we debate legal niceties, she's probably drifting into never-never land. To get her out, I need to know what happened to her. And I need to know now, not after some board meeting next week."

"Union contract clearly stipulates . . ."

"I don't give a damn about union contracts." Saul pointed a finger at the technician. While the lawyer had been learning the genteel art of jurisprudence inside a Harvard classroom, Saul had been prowling the back alleys of Cincinnati in a squad car practicing a much more potent method of upholding the law. "If that woman dies in there, you go down for manslaughter, and maybe spend the rest of your life breaking big rocks into little rocks at Leavenworth. You co-operate and there's a good chance I can get that woman out. Who you want to listen to? Your lawyer or me?"

The technician, who had never seen the inside of a prison, imagined them to resemble zoos crammed full of caged meat-eaters suffocating in the stench of their own waste, endlessly pacing back and forth while their keepers poked at them through steel bars. Surprisingly, for someone with no actual firsthand knowledge, he wasn't far wrong. "I'll answer your questions."

"My client will talk to you only off the record," said the lawyer speaking into his recorder. Life to him fell very cleanly into two categories. Preparing for prosecution, and preparing for defense. "And only in the interest of . . ."

Saul ignored him. "What happened?"

The technician leaned forward putting his left hand on his left knee, his right forearm on his right thigh, as though preparing to tell a close fishing buddy about the whopper that mysteriously got away. "I never saw anything like it. In training classes they give us these computerized simulations of what malfunctions look like. Well, this started out like she was overweight. Like she was heavier than she was supposed to be. The frequency needles dithered, and the timing pulses skipped a beat. Textbook example. Except it kept getting worse. Like there were two of her, or three even." He spread his hands a foot away from each other, reconsidered, then moved them as far apart as he could reach. "Like she was gigantic. Like we had missed her weight by a ton or more."

"You double-checked the scale?"

"First thing. It was right on the money. If I misweighed her, it wasn't by more than one one-hundredth of a gram. Peanuts."

"And you?" Saul addressed Galina's hostess. "You watched her until she disappeared?" It was standard operating procedure with celebrities.

"Yes, sir." Unlike the technician, she oozed composure. She had come to accept as reality her distorted image in the corporation's fun-house mirror. "There was absolutely nothing unusual about it. It went as smoothly as always up until the warning lights went on."

"Anything unusual about her? She seem suicidal or anything like that?" People had been known to try and alter their weight prior to transferring. Expiring inside the wires was reputedly one of the more pleasant ways to die.

"No, not really. She didn't talk much, and she seemed awfully nervous. Kind of preoccupied. But she was basically a pussycat. Not like celebrities usually. She followed instructions to the letter. No sass, no complaints."

"You noticed nothing out of the ordinary about her?"

"Except for her being so docile, no."

Saul turned to Ralph. "I'll want Herman and Rosie."

Ralph kept a notebook filled with the preferences of every higher-up he dealt with. Michelle Warren, for instance, took up two pages. Saul had two lines. One for Herman, one for Rosie.

Herman Lindstrom, a young, brilliant engineer, understood more about the technical aspects of matter transference than any other person alive. Rosie had second sight. An ability to penetrate the thin wall separating here from everywhere. She took no money for what she did. It was a God-given gift, she maintained, and therefore should not be sold. So, instead of paying her directly for her work, the Bridge Authority made regular donations to her Taos-based nonprofit foundation for the study of psychic healing.

"Rosie's in recovery now. She should be out in fifteen minutes. I have a limo standing by at the airport to pick up Herman."

Herman never set foot inside a bridge. The prospect of riding wire terrified him. He traveled everywhere by the old-fashioned method of flying. Needless to say, the Bridge Authority kept him well-isolated from the press.

Saul nodded and walked downstairs into the computer section, a matador about to do battle with an invisible bull.

CHAPTER 3

Meticulously, Saul checked the tapes of Galina Rosmanov's transfer, both the electrical impulse/methodology recordings and the videos. He didn't have enough technical expertise to evaluate them completely; Herman would do that later. Still, he was knowledgeable enough to make a general evaluation, and from what he could tell, the technician had been right. He had followed the proper procedures, pushed the correct buttons. The first hint of a malfunction had come only *after* Galina Rosmanov entered the wires, hence the trouble lay somewhere within the system's innards.

"You." Saul pointed to one of the engineers Ralph had standing by. "Confirm the origination of every passenger emerging within the past hour from out of any transportal with a direct energy linkup on this line." In the early days, before the Bridge Authority developed a foolproof insulation, transferees sometimes jumped wires, either hanging up inside a parallel line or popping out at the wrong terminal. But it hadn't happened for years, and Saul didn't hold much hope for it this time. "And don't neglect the privates," he added. There were six private transportals in the world. The U. S. President had two, one at the White House, one at the winter White House in Jacksonville. There was one in Moscow, one in Peking, and one at Michelle Warren's home in Big Sur. The sixth private transportal was located at Saul's villa estate in Chumpato, Guatemala.

Saul took the next engineer in line. "Run an energy level check on every exit terminal in the system." A formidable task. The Bridge Authority had transportals set up in every major city on earth. Outside the North American continent, the Bridge Authority operated through a licensing arrangement. Local entrepreneurs supplied the necessary terminal buildings and power. The Bridge Authority provided the equipment and the technicians. Other countries, notably Russia and Israel, had developed their own system of bridges, but their safety record was abominable. Both networks were constantly plagued by maintenance problems and technical malfunctions. The Bridge Authority refused to share the patented techniques that could have straightened them out. As a result, neither Russia nor Israel could gain a toehold in the extremely safety-conscious world market. "Look for unexplained energy surges. Start with this wire and move out relay link by relay link until you've covered them all. She may have come out, but may not have rematerialized. That's a real long shot, but it has happened.

"Start sifting collector stations," said Saul to another engineer. "The ones between here and Washington first. If they prove negative, see me and I'll tell you which ones to hit next." This chore would take by far the longest to accomplish, collector stations being the most complex links in the system. Sorting through the contents of one approximated examining each grain of sand on a wind-swept beach in search of the one trillion or so grains that had originally constituted the same boulder.

Saul addressed another engineer. "You inspect the fail safes." If power fizzled anywhere along the route, overlapping generators cut in and automatically rematerialized travelers at the nearest exit. It had happened only three times in Bridge Authority history, and the system had worked flawlessly in every instance. There was no hint that it had happened here; still it was a possibility and had to be considered.

"Check out the cargo wires." Saul indicated another of the engineers. "See if there's any evidence of a crossover." The Bridge Authority ran an extensive system of cargo bridges in addition to its passenger net. The only difference between the two nets was that the cargo transportals were larger to facilitate the entry of bigger crates, and the transmission process took a few microseconds longer because of the increased volumes involved. Many vacationers used the cargo bridges to transport both themselves and their cars. This increased the price of their tickets, but saved them the cost and hassle of renting a car when they arrived at their final destination, and spared them the aggravation of lugging their suitcases around and searching for a parking space at the terminal.

"You," Saul said to the next engineer, "you probe the military net." It was much larger than the civilian network and was restricted to use by military personnel. The chance of an inadvertent crossover was minuscule, still it was a contingency that had to be evaluated.

Saul tipped a cigarette out of his pack, lit it, and inhaled it deeply. That was it. All the starting points. Nothing left to do but wait and see what developed.

Suddenly Saul felt giddy and lightheaded, as though his problems had instantly vanished, as though he had just transitioned from winter to spring.

"Hello, Saul," said a voice behind him.

He turned to face Rosie. "Hello, sweetheart. You're looking good." He kissed her on the cheek. "Ralph brief you?"

She nodded.

"Have you pinpointed her yet?" Rosie's contribution to the extrication process was an ability to establish psychic contact with missing travelers.

Rosie's head bobbed up and down repeatedly, but that could indicate either an affirmation or simply another symptom of advancing age. "Mind if I take a seat, Saul? You know at sixty-eight the old pins don't hold you up the way they did at twenty." Rosie lowered herself onto the nearest chair. She stood only five three, yet weighed nearly two hundred pounds and seemed to get even heftier everytime Saul saw her. Considering the remarkable tranquillity individuals experienced in her presence, Saul had almost come to believe she grew larger by absorbing the bulk of other people's miseries. "Absolutely nothing, Saul. Not a glimmer, not a hint. Usually I can instantly locate them by homing in on their fear. It radiates from them the way heat shimmers from a block of newly scorched wood. But not this time. Here I get zero. It's as though this Rosmanov girl fell off the edge of the world."

"Sir," interrupted one of the engineers. "I ran an analysis on every exit gate."

"And?"

"Negative, sir. Checked and double-checked. Not a single unoriginated exit on any of them."

Shortly thereafter, two more engineers came over. No unexplained energy surges, said one. No sign of a foul-up in the fail safes, said the other.

The cargo wires and the military net also came up clean.

That left only the collector stations.

Saul called his engineers to him. "We've narrowed it to the collector stations. To save time, I want you to pair off and double-team them. The first man scans, the second rescans. Let me know the instant you find *anything*."

While Saul presided over the pairing-up, Rosie sat at a table toying with the deck of cards she always carried with her. She shuffled them, cut them three times, and flipped the top one over. Queen of hearts. Galina Rosmanov? She turned over another. Ace of spades. Death card. Rosie put it back into the deck, shuffled, looked at the top card, threw down the deck and stood. "I'm kind of tired, Saul. I think I'll catch a nap. Call me if you need me." She hobbled out into the hall.

When she had gone, Saul reached down and turned over the card she had seen last. Ace of spades. Again.

At that point, Herman Lindstrom arrived. As usual, he had a girl with him, a well-proportioned honey-blonde who gazed in awe at the hubbub surrounding her, obviously not understanding the significance of any of it. But then Herman, twenty-seven years old, with deep blue eyes, full pouting lips, and the chiseled features usually associated with Cinemascope screens and Saturday afternoon matinees, rarely chose his female companions for their intelligence. His type of women usually regarded their bodies as short-term, gilt-edged bonds, and considered each new wrinkle as an erosion of capital.

"What's up?" Herman asked.

Saul explained the situation as best he could.

Herman took no notes. Herman never took notes. He held scores of patents on improvements to the bridge network. The Bridge Authority used the Lindstrom Collector exclusively. Herman had shared the Nobel Prize with the MIT group that had constructed the first operating bridge. Yet Herman had never set so much as a single equation down on paper. He dictated his findings to assistants who transcribed them. The scholarly journals that published his work never bothered to evaluate it for significance or accuracy. When it came to matter transference, Herman was always in the forefront, and always right.

"What do you suggest?" Saul asked when he had finished his explanation.

Herman doodled his fingers across the top of a computer console. "If she's inside a collector, she'll stay intact for a little longer than she would in the wires proper. About twenty-four hours max. Unfortunately, inside a collector she'll be much harder to find. What it boils down to is that we can't screw around waiting for a collector-by-collector analysis."

That left only one alternative. "We send in the maintenance men?"

Herman slipped off his doeskin jacket, rolled up the sleeves on his tapered chambray shirt, and prepared to go to work. "You got it."

CHAPTER 4

In groups of three and four, the maintenance men entered the computer room. There were twenty-six of them total, slightly more males than females. They were young, on the average probably no more than twenty-four, and cocky. They milled around in small clusters, talking shop and joking among themselves, pointedly ignoring the other engineers present.

They had ample justification for their arrogance.

Maintenance men drew a base salary of $1,750,000 a year. Overtime and high-risk incentive pay pushed them far over the two-million-dollar mark and made them easily the Bridge Authority's highest-paid employees. Of course, for that kind of money, they performed the most dangerous job in the organization, quite possibly the most dangerous job in the world.

Their on-job mortality rate ran nearly 20 per cent per year.

The average maintenance man normally retired after only seventeen months on the job.

A near-legendary maintenance man named Gus Wiley held the informal record for maintenance longevity. Two months shy of six years. He became the subject of a full-length movie, a stage play, and a hit pop song. One day, about six months after he had retired, Gus Wiley went into the basement of his plush Beverly Hills mansion, stuck a loaded pistol into his mouth, and pulled the trigger. Twice. Maintenance men had fantastically quick reflexes.

Investigative journalists could not explain it. The man had been a hero. He had invested his salary wisely. He could have passed the rest of his life in comfort. He had everything to live for.

But his fellow maintenance men understood. They knew what it was like to ride wire at subnormal speed. Experiencing the rush that could never be duplicated by such mundane energizers as sex, liquor, or drugs. Inside the wires they were omnipresent, omnipotent, omniscient, omni-everything. Gods able to create a world according to their own parameters. Able to see colors, to touch sound. Able, also to peer into their own future and foresee the agony Gus Wiley had known, the agony of being too frightened of the wires to ever set foot inside one again.

They could understand only too well why he had killed himself. What recourse for a god permanently barred from heaven?

Saul rarely encountered a situation difficult enough to require employing the maintenance men. Each time he did, accounting would invariably send him a memo afterward pointing out that a full sweep by the maintenance men cost the Bridge Authority a goodly number of dollars in high-risk incentive pay. The first time the figure had been $550,000. What with inflation, a full sweep now went for close to a million two. Accounting's memos still crumpled down to the same size however. About an inch in circumference. Exactly the right heft for a perfect arch shot from Saul's desk to his wastebasket.

When the maintenance men were all present, Saul stood up before them and briefed them on the situation. Their job, he explained, would be to scour the system's collector stations, searching for any sign of the missing ballerina. Saul gave them each individualized computer printouts detailing their precise assignments.

They donned their specially built maintenance jackets, one by one stepped into the transportal, and disappeared.

Their jackets nullified the effects of the matter-transference process and slowed their transmission speed. The jackets also contained a microprocessor-based consolidation programmer, in effect a miniature collector station. As a result, maintenance men could traverse the system slowly from the inside with enough control over their mental and physical processes to make relatively major adjustments to the net's construction. Unfortunately, at such slow speeds, prolonged interwire contact with normally moving traffic would eventually disrupt any maintenance man remaining stationary for too long. It was, as the Bridge Authority characteristically understated, the prime disadvantage of the profession.

"What are their chances of finding her?" Saul asked Herman after the last maintenance man had disappeared.

"I honestly can't say," Herman responded. "Normally, if she was hung up in a collector station, their chances would be excellent. But this isn't a normal hang-up. I reran the records of her transfer fifty, maybe sixty times. I found nothing. Everything went exactly as it should have. She wasn't underweighed, the system performed flawlessly, there's no reason in the world why she shouldn't have popped out the other end."

"Except she didn't."

"Yes, except she didn't." Herman displayed the bewildered expression of a parent whose honor student child has just been arrested for grand theft auto. "I'll continue to run checks, but I really won't be able to do much more until I get their reports." He jerked a thumb toward the transportal indicating the maintenance men, even though most were no longer within a thousand miles of this room.

Saul settled back and did his best to endure the part of the process he despised most. The waiting. One of the reasons he worked so well with the bridges was because they so suited his personality. The mystery. The disastrous consequences likely to result from even the smallest error. But most of all the instantaneous action. He picked up a pocket beeper and left word with Herman that he was going to get something to eat.

He hailed a cab, not the easiest task since it was nearly two A.M., and rode to the pink zone where he entered La Bodega, his favorite Mexico City restaurant, a place where pretenses had long ago been trampled to the floor and covered with a thick layer of peanut shells and beer. He sat at the bar, ordered a Dos Equis to quench his thirst, and then switched to tequila straight.

After polishing off a fairly decent plate of sautéed prawns, he joined the band, a motley three-piece group of elderly men, one on violin, one on piano, one on guitar. He sang hopelessly off key in English, they sang almost as badly in Spanish. The spectators, mostly lower-class workers and a few tourists soaking up local color, applauded heartily after each number. The waiters pulled a few tables against the wall to clear an area for dancing.

Saul grabbed the nearest attractive female, a curvaceous, dark-eyed local girl, and launched into a mad polka. The girl laughed, clutched herself tightly to him, and followed his every move with vigorous good humor.

During one of the band's intermissions, she slipped the key to her apartment into his pocket. He took it out, smiled, nodded, and helped her on with her coat. He left her in the foyer while he hailed a cab. It had just arrived when his pocket beeper sounded. He clicked its volume up and held it to his ear.

"Go ahead," he said.

"They're coming back," Herman informed him.

"Be right there," said Saul.

He slipped into the taxi, gave the driver the address of the Mexico City terminal and promised him a five-hundred-peso tip if he could make it in less than fifteen minutes.

Only several days later, when his laundry woman showed him the strange key that had fallen out in the wash did he remember the dusky señorita who had stood in La Bodega's doorway, hurling Spanish curses after him at the top of her ample lungs.

The maintenance men drifted back one by one, with distressingly similar reports. No results. Negative. Nothing.

"What do you make of it?" Saul asked Herman after the last maintenance man had returned.

"I don't know. It's got me stumped." To Herman, a challenge supreme. He hunched over his computer terminal and settled down for a long bout of serious keypunching.

Saul's phone rang. His assigned secretary answered. "Yes, ma'am," she said. "Right away." She hung up and hailed Saul.

"Sir, it's Miss Warren. She's upstairs in the city director's office, and would like you to report to her there at once."

For as long as Saul had known Michelle, for as long as she had been president of the Bridge Authority, even in the direst of emergencies her employees always came to her. Saul had never once seen her venture into the computer room or the maintenance sectors, areas she called the bowels of the organization and treated accordingly.

Reluctantly, Saul entered the elevator and began his trip to a higher level.

CHAPTER 5

"You're looking well, Saul." Michelle escorted her exhusband into the city director's office. At a glance, Saul took in the familiar trappings that always accompanied her presence. Her Saks Fifth Avenue coat hung casually across a chair. Her pigskin attaché case rested open atop the director's coffee table. Her correspondence lay in neatly ordered rows on the director's desk. Her scent, a combination of expensive French perfume and raw animal musk, filled the room with the barest hint of ultimate but unattainable pleasure.

She pecked Saul lightly on the cheek, the kiss of casual friends and past lovers. He plodded heavily to one of the director's plush easy chairs and sat down. Like a magnet being shoved away by the similar polarity of another, Michelle chose a chair on the other side of the office, as far from Saul as she could possibly get. "What's going on down there?" She tamped tobacco into the bowl of her blue-enameled pipe. It bore her initials on one side, the Bridge Authority logo on the other. A company woman straight down the line.

"Got a real puzzler this time." Saul lit a cigarette and searched for an ashtray. When he found none within immediate reach, he dropped his match unceremoniously onto the director's thick pile carpeting. He had no respect whatsoever for the trappings of executive power. Plush offices reminded him of pet-shop fish tanks where colored gravel, bright greenery, and shining tinsel paper gave the tiniest of minnows the appearance of sharks.

"So Ralph tells me. How bad is it?" Michelle sat with her back to a display of early bridge advertising, stuff the Bridge Authority had spent millions producing to convince people to trust themselves to something totally beyond their comprehension. Large ads, double-paged and extremely factual, they contained scientific testimony, running tallies of accident-free miles, and blobs of mathematical equations liberally interspersed throughout words and graphs like the droppings of an erudite chicken.

But that was the early stuff.

The current Bridge Authority ad campaign stressed the money-saving advantages of traveling midweek. Individual ads devoted not so much as a subordinate paragraph to safety. But then, why should they? Nobody worried about accidents anymore.

At least not until somebody like Galina Rosmanov came along and proved that maybe they should.

"It's as bad as possible. We can't find her."

"You what?" Michelle leaned forward incredulously, setting off ripples of light in her sunshine-colored hair. "You can't find her? That's absurd." Seldom having experienced failure in her own life, Michelle found it extremely difficult to comprehend how it could happen to others. Hard work, tenacity, a bit of ruthlessness should overcome any obstacle. At least they had in Michelle's case.

She had worked her way through Sarah Lawrence (a B.A.), Harvard Law School (an L.L.B.), and UCLA (an M.B.A.). Just as Western marshals pinned their five-pointed stars to the outside of their vests to cow potential troublemakers with a visible emblem of their authority, so Michelle kept her diplomas tacked on prominent display on her office wall.

She had joined the Bridge Authority as a statistician, and had quickly risen through the ranks to vice-president of marketing. It was shortly after attaining that post that she made the only mistake of her life. She culminated three love-filled vacation weeks in Europe with a bridge-ride to a Reno wedding chapel in the company of Saul Lukas.

They couldn't have been more incompatible. She drank tequila sunrises and dusty wine. Saul took his liquor straight. He couldn't differentiate between Gallo Hearty Burgundy and a '72 Beulieu Zinfandel, both of which he drank out of tumblers with ice. Around the house Michelle wore Gucci lounging robes and Capezio slippers. Saul padded about in cutoff Levi's, canvas Adidas, and one of the old, sleeveless UCLA sweatshirts she kept around for dusting the furniture.

Her friends and business acquaintances frequently remarked that she resembled Saul's parole officer more than his wife. They nicknamed her Warden.

She began working nights, purposely arriving home long after Saul had already gone to bed. And she was secretly quite relieved when one of her friends blurted out that Saul was having an affair with a rising movie starlet.

Their divorce made every society page in the country. She got the bulk of the estate, everyone's sympathy, and full social absolution for her temporary excursion outside the bounds of her status. And she resumed her maiden name.

On the day her decree became final, her friends threw her a coming-out party. In the weeks thereafter, she held frequent open houses, trying in vain to fill a score of empty rooms with two score of even emptier acquaintances. Although she would admit it to no one, not even to her analyst, she had loved Saul, and sometimes, especially when besieged by the incessant babble of suitors who regarded the courting dance as a formal minuet rather than a frenzied tango, loved him still.

Saul took nothing when he moved out except his clothing—one suitcase easily held every shred—her UCLA sweatshirt, and a bone pendant bearing a blue scrimshaw butterfly, which Michelle had purchased for him on their honeymoon in Mendocino. He still wore it sometimes to remind himself how quickly good things can end.

"I know it sounds crazy," Saul responded, "but we can't find her."

"What about Lindstrom? Surely he can provide an answer." Typical Michelle logic. Your watch broken? Take it to a jeweler. Got a problem in the wires? Go see a scientist.

"He was trying to figure it out when I left him to come up here. Rosie can't get a fix on her either," Saul added as an afterthought.

"I'm surprised she admits it for a change," Michelle said sarcastically. "You know, Saul, accounting cringes everytime I authorize a check to that pseudoscientific foundation of hers. Everybody in this organization considers that woman a complete charlatan. Everybody but you."

"Michelle, I've seen healers at that foundation straighten twisted legs, restore sight, relieve pain."

"Psychosomatic illnesses. There was nothing wrong with those people to begin with."

"I saw a healer there mend a broken arm. Was that psychosomatic, too?"

"She only affirms what you want to hear."

"So what? Suppose Rosie does fake her readings? Suppose she can't tell any more from the whirls of energy around her than a gypsy can from the sediment in the bottom of a teacup? So what? The point is, she fulfills a need. Take a look at the world around you. What do you see? Depersonalization. Automation. Everything ticking along according to strict, unchanging, scientifically precise rules. Know what's missing from this world? Intrigue. Magic. The arcane enigma. And people need it. They need something that works for no apparent reason, something that works simply because they believe it will. They need that something so badly that if someone were to set up a medical school and turn out the Western equivalent of witch doctors, it wouldn't be long before those doctors would have their diplomas hanging like talismans on office walls along Park Avenue. And you, and your scoffing, high-class friends would be going to them and wearing feathers in your hair and carrying bouquets of dried ginseng root and drinking potions of powdered bat's blood and swearing they brought you relief from your peptic ulcers and your tennis elbows and your chronic impotence." Saul fished in his pocket and brought out another cigarette. "Now would you mind if we got back to Galina Rosmanov?"

"I don't think that will be necessary."

"I don't follow you." Saul's cigarette dangled from his mouth, his lighter flickering in front of it like some miniature eternal flame marking the grave of a martyr who had searched in vain for justice.

"You said yourself you couldn't find her anywhere in the wires."

"So what."

"That would lead me to believe she is no longer in the wires, and therefore no longer our problem. I say we hang it on the Mexican government, dump it into their lap, and extricate ourselves from the matter completely. I mean it's not as if we wouldn't have ample precedent."

She had a point there.

More people got fatally lost going out of Mexico City than got lost out of all the other Bridge Authority terminals combined. Oddly enough, most of these Mexico City losses tended to be low-level diplomats, embassy public affairs co-ordinators, cultural attachés, titles that had become synonymous over the years with intelligence agent.

The official story was that this disproportionate number of disappearances was simply a result of Mexican incompetence, a highly unlikely explanation since few nationals operated as technicians in any country. Most, in fact, were American, imported by the Bridge Authority expressly to run the net and transferred often throughout the system.

The unofficial story maintained that Mexico City had, by illicit consensus, become a free zone for political assassination. There were widely circulating rumors of bribes to technicians and more than one instance of sabotaged weighing equipment, but the whole process still remained shadowed in speculation. Certainly any consolidated and ongoing plot would have required the complicity and tacit approval of the Bridge Authority, yet Michelle consistently denied any knowledge of it whenever Saul raised the issue. Nevertheless, he made a mental note to check out fully Galina Rosmanov's political background at his earliest opportunity.

"Look," Saul countered, "of the people we've lost before, we've either brought them out in one piece, dead or alive, or they've dissipated before we could extricate them. But we've always been able to find them. Always. This is a totally unique situation, and I'm not going to kiss it off without finding out what happened in those wires."

"I could order you to. I am your superior, you know." She said it as though she were commenting on the sunrise, the onset of autumn, or any other of the world's invariable certainties.

"You do that and I'll lay out so much bad publicity your revenue graphs will look like the first big drop on a roller coaster."

"That's blackmail."

"Whatever it takes to get the job done."

Half of Michelle's mouth turned down, half turned up, as though she couldn't decide whether to laugh or to cry. "Get out of here. Go back downstairs with the rest of the weirdos and freaks."

It was the first order she had ever given Saul that he was glad to carry out.

CHAPTER 6

Herman sat at the data terminal keyboard banging out programs with the virtuosity and gusto of a ragtime piano player in a speakeasy.

"Any luck?" Saul asked him.

Herman waited for one last piece of punched paper tape to clatter out of his reader. He studied it, frowned, and let it flutter to the ground. "Total blank." Herman snapped off the terminal and stood. "Old age must be creeping up on me," he said, vigorously shaking his arms. "Getting poor circulation."

Saul opened his briefcase, an ancient leather satchel secured with two straps, and brought out a fifth of Jack Daniels Red Label. He poured some into two glasses and passed one to Herman. Herman reached for it. His hand fluttered so badly he had to bring his other hand across to steady it.

"You've really got it bad, haven't you?" Saul said. "Maybe we should call in a doctor."

"No need. I've just been working too hard lately. I'm overtired, but I'll make it." Using both hands, he put his glass to his lips and downed half his liquor in one gulp. His shakiness perceptibly diminished. "See." He extended a rock-steady hand. "A touch of tonic and I'm good as new." He held out his glass for a refill. "What went on upstairs?"

Saul poured them both another healthy belt. "Michelle ordered me to drop it. Hang it on the Mexicans and let it go."

"I hope you didn't buy off."

"What do you think?"

Herman went to a nearby control panel. A multitude of tiny blips moved across the panel's tracer screen. Each of these blips indicated a passenger somewhere in wire transit between Mexico City and Washington, D.C. "I think Michelle's going to really scream when she hears what I propose we do next."

"Oh-oh. Sounds like good old Saul goes back into the pit for another round with the bulldog. What do you have in mind?"

Herman flipped a switch and the tracer screen died out. "I want to stop all traffic in the network. The sum effect will be an increase in our instruments' sensitivity. We'll be able to fine-tune on the slightest remaining particles."

Saul studied the darkened screen. "How long would we be out of commission?"

"Until we find her. It could be as short as an hour, or as long as a week."

"I didn't think anyone could stay intact in the wires for a week."

"Normally not. But without the disrupting influence of other traffic, who knows? It's something that's never happened before."

"How about halting traffic only between here and Washington?"

"One problem. I suspect she may have slipped out into another bridge. By now she could be anywhere in the system."

Saul glanced at the intricate, multicolored worldwide route map on the wall. Was it worth totally disrupting global economics to disentangle a nineteen-year-old Russian toe dancer from this electronic spider web?

"Rosie," Saul said, "you pick up anything yet?"

Rosie sat in a corner with her eyes half shut and her hands folded palms up in her lap, rocking back and forth in the Barcalounger Saul had secured for her. "No psychic impression. I do have a gut feeling, though." She nodded toward the transportal. "I think she's still in there. I think you ought to do what Herman says."

"I agree." Saul pushed his fingers through his close-cropped hair. "Now comes the hard part. Getting Michelle to go along. She doesn't see her passengers as people, you know." He rang for the elevator. "She sees them as endless progressions of dollar signs, as inanimate bags of money to be shuffled around and ticked off on her fingers."

The elevator arrived, and Saul stepped inside.

Michelle was not alone. She introduced the man with her as Nikolei Bulgavin, the Russian Secretary of Foreign Affairs. Saul kept current enough with politics to realize Bulgavin was widely reputed to be the sub rosa head of the Russian secret police. "Secretary Bulgavin will personally follow our progress in the Rosmanov matter," Michelle told Saul. "You can speak freely in front of him."

"I'm afraid I don't have much to report. We still haven't found her." He lobbed out the bombshell. "Herman suggests we halt all traffic in the network until we do."

"Halt all traffic?" Michelle drummed on the top of her desk with a pencil, gradually increasing her cadence from the hesitant tap of a blind man's cane to the assured staccato of a runaway machine gun. "Halt all traffic? That's impossible. We'd lose millions every hour if we did that. Not to mention the total disruption it would cause in world commerce. Do you have any idea how many people we put through the wires in an average day? Millions. No, I'm afraid we can't do that."

Saul turned to Bulgavin. Here, at least, he would have an ally. "Perhaps we should consult with Secretary Bulgavin before we go writing off one of his countrymen."

But Bulgavin surprised Saul. "I'm afraid I must agree with Miss Warren." He extended his hand to Michelle, palm up, fingers open, the way a magician would to prove himself completely free of hidden rabbits. "Since apparently you have been able to find no trace of Galina, we are prepared to accept reluctantly the unfortunate conclusion that she has expired without a trace. I will inform the newspapers that we hold the Bridge Authority blameless, that her disappearance was a quirk of providence." He smiled. His false teeth fit so badly Saul half suspected he had instructed his state dentist to make them that way on purpose in order to enhance his already considerable resemblance to a rabid jackal. "Will such a statement be acceptable to the Bridge Authority, Miss Warren?"

"Quite acceptable," Michelle replied, "and most generous, indeed. On behalf of the Bridge Authority I will draft up a response expressing our sympathies for your country's profound artistic and personal loss. Naturally our insurance company will be in touch."

"Naturally." Bulgavin reached out his hand to shake hers.

"I think we're being a wee bit hasty shoveling dirt over the coffin," Saul interjected, "especially since we may not yet have a corpse. To repeat, Herman says if we stop all traffic, there's a chance we can find Galina Rosmanov alive."

Michelle swung her delicate hands in front of her like two inverted pendulums. "I really don't want to carry this conversation any further," she said testily. "My decision has been made."

"The profound economic disruptions involved with stopping the entire network do not seem to justify the extremely low probabilities of success." Bulgavin spoke with the hasty rationality of a public bureaucrat anxious to avoid having to work past quitting time.

"You know," said Saul, "the Federal Transportation Agency might disagree with you both. They seem to have a profound sympathy for the plight of the passenger, a sympathy I sense might be missing here."

The Federal Transportation Agency. The one threat that might conceivably carry weight with Michelle. In the early days of matter transference, there were many unconfirmed reports of malfunctions and bungled transmissions. The overwhelming feeling at the time was that the technology involved in the bridges was far too complex to turn bridge operation over to general industry. So the government set up the Bridge Authority as a monopolistic public utility under the Federal Transportation Agency. In reality, the Bridge Authority operated autonomously. But that autonomy could end in an instant should the FTA ever decide to assert its legally sanctioned jurisdiction. "Let me discuss it with Secretary Bulgavin," Michelle told Saul. "In private."

Saul left the office. Several minutes later, Michelle called him back. Bulgavin was no longer there. He had left by the side door in Saul's absence. "That was a pretty crude maneuver," said Michelle. "You know we do pay your ticket. You are in our employ. When we yank your chain, you're not supposed to bite our ankle."

"I like to think of myself as acting director of corporate morals. It seems to be an open position at the moment. What did you and the good Secretary decide?"

"I'll shut down the wires."

"Good decision."

"But only on an hour-to-hour basis. You give me a progress report every sixty minutes. The instant I decide it's hopeless—I repeat, the instant *I* decide it's hopeless—we go back on the line immediately. Clear?"

"Perfectly." He turned and walked out of her office. Neither one bothered saying good-by.

"We go off the line," Saul told Herman.

Herman nodded and immediately set to work making the necessary arrangements.

"Was it much of a hassle?" asked Rosie.

"Indeed it was. You know, it's funny," Saul said, "but the people upstairs seem especially anxious to knock this one off. I'm beginning to suspect this whole affair may have political overtones. The question is, How to find out for sure?" Saul wrapped a long strand of punched paper tape around his hand. When he looked at the results, he noticed he could still glimpse isolated patches of skin through the places where several holes accidentally lined up. "Rosie, what say you and me go take a look at Galina Rosmanov's apartment."

CHAPTER 7

Amid an intensive public relations barrage highlighting the Bridge Authority's great civic-minded nature and extreme concern for the safety of its passengers, the entire wire network went into an unprecedented emergency standby mode. Only those individuals directly engaged in the attempt to clear the wires and restore the system to full service were allowed to pass through.

On their way to the predeparture gates, Saul and Rosie passed hundreds of stranded passengers all of whom were standing fast, banking on a swift resolution to the crisis. "I hope they're right," said Saul as he and Rosie entered the predeparture door marked Rome.

Shortly after Italy went communistic, the Russians had invaded it with an army of scientists, athletes, and government officials. A domicile in Italy became a reward for loyal party service, an official recognition of a worthwhile contribution to the political cause. In qualitative terms Italy came to occupy the linear extreme counterbalanced on the other end by Siberia.

Most Russian artists chose to live in Florence; scientists in Milan; athletes in Sicily. Russia's government officials lived in Rome. And so did Galina Rosmanov.

Saul and Rosie took their recovery capsules and stepped, in turn, Rosie first, into the transportal.

An hour later, Saul hailed them a cab for the drive into the city. The ride would take seventy-five minutes, longer than the trip from Mexico City, but that seemed to be the hidden clinker with any new mode of transportation. To take advantage of cheap land and beneficent zoning regulations, terminals always came to be located far outside the cities they served. It had happened with airlines and again with the bridges.

But in this case, Saul didn't really mind. He hadn't been in Rome since the Communists rose to power, and he was anxious to see if it had changed.

Unfortunately, the answer was yes. The Russians had stripped it bare of art and statuary, which they had then transported piece by piece back to the Motherland. Even the fabled fountains of Rome and been dismantled. The Trevi Fountain now spouted water in Red Square where visitors tossed rubles into it to assure their eventual return to Moscow. The Hermitage displayed the art works that had once graced Roman squares and pediments. Michelangelo's statue of Marcus Aurelius now guarded the entrance to the Kremlin.

But at least these works, even though brazenly plundered from their native land, would survive. Not so the monumental relics of the glory that had been Rome. Regarding them as remembrances of an undesirable democratic past, the Russians had set about demolishing them and replacing them with symbols of a better socialistic future. A housing collective occupied the former site of the Colosseum. A medical center replaced the Forum. The catacombs made ideal air-raid shelters. Vatican City became a missile complex, silos and gantries replacing crucifixes on a nearly one-for-one basis.

The free world issued vigorous protests against this rape of democratic heritage. The Russians commented only once, and only in a most chillingly roundabout manner. Party Chief Sokrav speaking with French Prime Minister Galarneau at a cocktail reception for the African Ambassador had stated that if turmoil did not cease regarding, as he put it, "this Italian affair," the Eiffel Tower, the Statue of Liberty, and St. Paul's Cathedral would fall next.

Turmoil ceased. So Italy had given the free world music, art, and political ideals. Had it not also produced the Mafia, Mussolini, and the spaghetti western? Why risk a world war to preserve a culture as ambivalent as that? And thus, typically, the world's liberals had folded their tents and stolen away into the comforting night of a less directly threatening cause.

The doorman in Galina's apartment building wore a Russian Army uniform with six progressively shorter rows of plastic ribbons laddered above his heart. The gleam of his brass buttons had begun to cloud over like the eyes of an old tomcat that had entered one alley squabble too many. He spoke perfect English, but refused to admit it until Saul slipped him a generous tip. Once he had money firmly in hand, he gladly escorted Saul and Rosie to the top floor and, with his passkey, admitted them to the penthouse suite.

Galina's apartment could easily have belonged to 90 per cent of the world's single working girls. It certainly contained the correct common denominators. A breakfast table with two chairs. A stiff-backed sofa and matching easy chair of the type decorating books led women to believe gives a room a firm anchor. An expensive Japanese stereo with exceptionally bad fidelity. Records evenly split between classics and current American pop. A bed large enough to comfortably accommodate two so long as the double occupancy lasted no more than a few hours.

The refrigerator held two bottles of good French wine and a varied assortment of diet salad dressings. The lettuce inside the crisper had started to brown around the edges. Every potato in the vegetable bin had begun to sprout. Green mold covered the cheese; the meat was turning black. Clearly, Galina Rosmanov wasn't much for cooking in.

"What are we looking for?" Rosie asked. She opened a bureau drawer and thumbed through its contents, a filmy assortment of translucent lingerie. She removed a flimsy brassiere and held it to her breast. It barely reached halfway across. Carefully she refolded the garment and returned it precisely to its place, treating it with the care of a yellowed yet familiar photograph lifted out of an album depicting her own somewhat frivolous youth.

"Anything out of the ordinary," Saul answered. "Anything which might give us a clue as to who might not want Galina Rosmanov to walk out the other end of a bridge." Saul drew a blank in the kitchen and in the living room.

His luck changed considerably in the den, however.

Behind a small but apparently original Picasso etching he discovered a safe. He tugged at the handle. Locked. "Hey, Rosie," he yelled into the bedroom. "How are you at psyching out safe combinations?"

She stuck her head into the room. "Terrific. Try eighty-five left, sixteen right, thirty left."

"You kidding?"

"Try them and see."

Saul did. The safe popped open. "My God, Rosie. That was amazing. How did you do it?"

She waddled across the floor toward him. "Simple. I pulled the drawer out of her nightstand and found those three numbers written out on a piece of paper taped to the bottom." She grinned broadly. "In addition to being one of the all-time great psychics, I am probably the world's leading fan of TV detective shows. I can toss an apartment like a pro. Believe me, if I could conjure safe combinations out of the air like that, I would have retired long ago." She turned her face skyward. "Only kidding up there," she said sprightly.

Saul reached into the safe and pulled out its contents. A spiral notebook filled with technical equations, an amber plastic vial with a white safety cap and a cork-stoppered clear-glass bottle half-full of chalky white powder. The vial held about fifty grayish aspirin-sized tablets. Saul sniffed one. It had a mildly pungent aroma, like a mixture of honey and cloves. None of the tablets carried any identifying markings. They were all slightly different in size, as though they had been made by hand. The powder had no discernible odor.

"You think she was mixed up in some kind of drug ring?" asked Rosie.

"Possible," said Saul. "Only one way to find out for sure."

While Rosie returned directly to Mexico City, Saul detoured through New York where he dropped the tablets and the powder off for analysis at the Bridge Authority's lab.

Immediately upon reviving in Mexico City, he went to see Herman. "Made any progress?" he asked.

"I think so," said Herman. "I'm picking up a strange permutation at the first collector station between here and Washington. I was just on my way out there for a closer look. Want to come?"

"How long will it take?"

"About an hour by light plane."

Saul looked at his desk. He hadn't reported to Michelle for

nearly five hours. He had at least six messages from her piled up atop his desk. Each of them carried the same words. SEE ME. URGENT!

He crumbled them up and dropped them into a wastebasket.

"Let's get going."

Each collector station signified the end of a bridge sector and, correspondingly, the beginning of a new one. A multilevel computer chain would take a traveler into the collector, another would take him out. Naturally these chains overlapped with enough redundancy to insure complete safety and to prevent on-stream collisions.

The collector station itself consisted of hundreds of huge metal spheres enclosed in a climatically stable building. It was the one place where matter transference had a physical representation. Every time a traveler passed through one of these spheres, the sphere pinged. Old-timers maintained they could listen to the strength of that ping and gauge to the nearest gram the weight of the traveler involved. The new breed scoffed at such unscientific assertions, choosing to use multimillion dollar instruments to accomplish the same task.

After introducing himself to the station's chief engineer, Herman sat down at the station's control console, hooked up several of the microprocessor-based test instruments he had brought with him, and began his scan.

After nearly an hour, he clicked the instruments off. "I can't be sure," he said, "but I think she's in there. Although I've never gotten a reading like this before. It's as if her weight has been increased at least threefold. Like somehow two other travelers had gotten tangled up with her. It's flat out impossible, but it would explain why we couldn't find her. We were searching for a scattered bunch of pebbles, not the Rocky Mountains."

"What happens now?"

"More tests, evaluations. It's still a bit premature to tell for sure. And like I say, I've never seen anything to quite compare to what this seems to be."

"What if it is her? Will you be able to extricate her?"

Herman rubbed a finger against his temple, as though trying to massage more information out of his brain. "Hard to say. We can't get an accurate reading on her weight once she's inside, and without that information, I really can't predict what we'll be able to do."

Saul clasped Herman's shoulder. "Keep plugging, buddy. If anybody can do it, you can. I only wish I could stick around and give you moral support, but I'm afraid I can't stall Michelle much longer."

He started to go and then remembered the spiral notebook in his briefcase. He pulled it out and showed it to Herman. "I found this in Galina Rosmanov's apartment. You have any idea what those notations mean?"

Herman looked at it, thumbed through it slowly, and handed it back. "Nothing significant. A few random notations on hydroelectronics. Probably the work of a student."

"Now what would she be doing with something like that?"

"Beats me." Suddenly, without warning, Herman doubled over.

Saul ran to him, helped him to a nearby lounge, and stretched him out on a sofa. "I don't care what you say," Saul told him. "We're getting a doctor in here right now."

"No." Laboriously Herman sat up. "I'll be O.K. It's just a cramp. Probably got hold of a bad sandwich."

"You're going to see a doctor."

"Sure. But not now. Later. As soon as I wrap this one up. Please, Saul. It's really important to me. O.K.? Later?"

This was the kind of choice Saul hated worst of all, the choice between friendship and duty. Without Herman's brilliance to guide them, there was no telling how long it would take the Bridge Authority's regular corps of engineers to get Galina Rosmanov out. On the other hand, Herman obviously needed medical attention, possibly even hospitalization. Which way to go? Of course, Saul went the way he always went. Duty every time. "Promise? You'll see a doctor as soon as we get her out?"

"Sure." Herman gave Saul his best boyish not-a-care-in-the-world grin. "And you ever know me to break a promise?"

"No, I never have." But somehow Saul felt that this time it might be different, though for the life of him he couldn't figure out why.

CHAPTER 8

Jackson, Michelle's new personal secretary, a young man with the muscular body of a serious weight lifter, called to mind a German shepherd Saul had known once. The dog had belonged to a federal prison guard. It had padded slavishly along at the guard's heels, reaching up often to lick its master's hand. No mental giant, the only skill the dog had ever been able to learn was, on command, to break a human wrist with a single shake of its powerful jaws. One skill. But all it had needed to see it comfortably through an entire lifetime.

Jackson informed Michelle via intercom that Saul was waiting to see her. She responded that she would be a minute. Saul lit a cigarette and sat down to wait.

"They tell me," Jackson said, "that you and Michelle used to be husband and wife."

Saul's words jabbed like invisible uppercuts into his exhaled smoke. "I think mongoose and cobra comes closer."

"I don't follow." Jackson tilted his head, as though by realigning his ears he could ease the flow of information into his meager brain. Saul wondered how fast he could type.

"I said yes, we used to be husband and wife."

"That's what I heard. Must be tough getting dumped by a swell lady like that."

Since Jackson didn't seem likely to be overly concerned with the emotional grief of a total stranger, his comment obviously carried a deeper implication, one Saul should have guessed. Expensive jewelry. Stylish clothes. But most of all the premature lines crinkling the secretary's face like tiny whip marks left there by repeated lashings with the end of a sharpened tongue.

"Tell you what. I'll give you a free bit of advice," said Saul. "If you want to have a long, tranquil relationship with Michelle, wash your hands at least twice an hour and don't spill pizza on her satin sheets."

Jackson nodded with the uncomprehending agreement of a spring-necked plastic bird bobbing in an auto's rear window.

"Jackson," said Michelle, "I'll see Mr. Lukas now."

Michelle sat at her desk, her arms outstretched in front of her. She wore a clingy blue dress custom designed for her by one of New York's finest couturiers. She had her hair done up in an intricate style, which suggested three hours in the care of a very expensive beautician. She looked flawless, but then she always looked flawless. Saul could count on one hand the instances he had ever seen her unkempt. In fact, he often told her he could scarcely tell the difference between her and their self-cleaning oven.

Saul pointed toward her secretary. "A poodle would eat less and probably provide a higher level of conversation."

"But could it do as many tricks?" Her smile might have been picked at random out of a box of cherry-filled paraffin lips. Full of sweetness but totally false. "Let's get straight to the point. The net has been closed for almost twenty-four hours. World trade has ground to a near halt. Airlines, trains, and buses cut back too far when the bridges came in. They can't handle the volume of traffic they used to. The last estimate I had said there was nearly eight million travelers still stranded in isolated terminals around the world. The Dow Jones today fell nearly 300 points to close below 2000 for the first time in years. I've gotten personal calls from the commerce and transportation secretaries of every major country. We are losing millions in revenue every hour. My stockholders are on my back. I can't hold off reopening the net much longer. Have you made any headway?"

"Yes. Herman thinks he's got Galina isolated in the first collector station between here and Washington."

"How soon before you get her out?"

"Hard to say. Apparently her weight was upped. How we don't know. How *much* we don't know either. That's the next thing we have to find out."

"So I expect that means you want me to keep the system closed."

"To the contrary. Herman says to resume traffic everywhere except between here and Washington."

Even before he had the last word out, she already had her phone in hand and had dialed the number of her chief operations officer. "When can I open that leg and be back into full service?" she asked Saul across the phone's mouthpiece.

Saul went to the window and looked out at Mexico City stretched below him. He could see the Reforma and off in the distance Chapultapec Park bathed in sunshine beneath the cheery, cloudless sky. When was the last time he had walked through a park in the sunshine? Years, perhaps. He was abruptly struck by the frightening prospect that he was becoming just another human mole, paid to scamper through the Bridge Authority's corporate burrows with the rest of the semiblind creatures of darkness. "You never look on the bright side, do you? You're never happy with partial success."

"No, I'm not, sweetheart. Tell me the truth, are you?" Her chief operations officer came on the phone. "Otto," she said, "good news. We're almost totally back on the line."

"So what happens next?" she asked Saul after she had spoken to the Bridge Authority's head of public relations to arrange for maximum press coverage of the system's reactivation.

Saul offered her a cigarette, which she refused, preferring to light up one of her own, instead. Its blue-tinted paper perfectly matched her dress. "I have a theory," he said. "I think somebody with a lot of technological juice is trying to ice Galina Rosmanov."

Michelle's cigarette wheeled back and forth between her thumb and forefinger like a tiny steamroller. "That's ridiculous. What could she have done to antagonize the big boys? I doubt they would become incensed over a bad Swan Lake."

"Right. That's why I think she's mixed up with something political." He pressed his lips into the tight grimace that invariably precedes a generous swig from a bottle of bitter medicine. "I'm going to check out the ballet company she danced with. I'd like you to go with me."

Michelle's eyes opened wide, then closed to narrow, guarded slits. "Why?"

"I'll need your help."

"If so, it will be the first time."

"I want you to translate for me."

"Sorry, hon. I don't speak Russian."

"I wasn't referring to language."

She had him in an uncomfortable position and wasn't about to let him easily off the hook. "In other words, you want me along for my quote cultural expertise unquote. Because I dress for dinner, don't slurp coffee out of my saucer, and support educational television."

"That's about the size of it, yes."

"Too bad we couldn't have formed this alliance five years ago. We could have coauthored an article for one of the true romance magazines. 'How ballet and a possible murder turned us into a team and saved our marriage.'" She slipped on her coat and followed Saul out the door.

They arrived at the Kennedy Center six hours before the opening of *Romeo and Juliet*.

The ballet master, Sergei Popovich, a trim, darkhaired man in his forties, was frantically rehearsing the young ballerina who would be dancing in Galina Rosmanov's place.

Saul and Michelle approached him. "Mr. Popovich," said Saul, "I'm Saul Lukas and this is Michelle Warren. I phoned from Mexico City about Galina Rosmanov."

"Yes, yes. From the American Bridge Authority." Popovich never took his eyes off his troupe. "No, no, no!" he shouted at his lead danseur. "You attack the arabesque with grace and style. A leap of freedom, not a jump in the air."

The young ballerina partnering the danseur executed a perfect gargouillade, spinning around as though she were perched atop a music box and covered with a Plexiglas dome.

"Isn't she beautiful," said Popovich. "And still only sixteen. I discovered her in a small ballet school in Volgograd. You shall hear great things about her. Mark my words."

"Did you discover Galina Rosmanov, too?" asked Saul.

"Ah, Galina. A brilliant *artiste*. But not one of mine. No. My predecessor. Gregor Alexian. He was . . . shall we say *relieved* of his position for his unorthodox beliefs. Poor Gregor. He maintained that his dancers must be given the freedom to express themselves however they may choose, with little if any restraint." Popovich punched his ballerina on the shoulder with his walking stick. "Down lower, and then swoop upward. The movement will seem more impressive for the contrast." He held the stick in both hands as if he were a samurai warrior ready to decapitate any dancer deviating in the slightest from his wishes.

"You don't believe that artists should be given freedom of expression?" asked Michelle.

"Of course not," he said as though lecturing a backward student on the fundamentals of arithmetic. "We must not let personal idiosyncracies encroach on tradition. No, in ballet as in all forms of art things must be done according to state policy. In a certain fashion, according to a certain order. To alter that fashion, to go beyond that order is, to say the least, unwise."

"And to say the most," Saul interjected, "potentially deadly?"

Popovich tucked his stick under one arm and clapped his hands in time to the music, giving his dancers a strong rhythm. "To say the most," he agreed almost inaudibly.

"Did Galina Rosmanov go beyond that order?" asked Michelle.

"Galina Rosmanov was a confused girl, a child really, with a child's stubbornness. A difficult dancer to control. But also a realist. She knew that to become a prima ballerina she must conform. So she did. Although she constantly strived to retain a semblance of individuality despite it."

Sounded like Saul's kind of lady. "I've heard rumors," he said, "she was about to defect. Any truth to that?"

Popovich signaled his dancers to take a break. "Unfortunately, Galina squandered her energy on what you call the fast life. Her dance suffered as a result. I had to caution her repeatedly to watch her timing. Her moves lost their precision, their power. I discussed this with her only the day before she left Mexico City. I told her that if she did not bear down and devote herself completely to her work, I would have to downgrade her to corps de ballet. Our discussion became quite heated at that point. She mentioned defection, but only in the way a child would talk about running away from home. As a device to elicit sympathy. Without any real intention of following through. I have a recent rehearsal film of her dancing a segment from *Ophelia*. I think if you watch it, you will see what I mean about her faltering technique."

Sergei handed them over to an assistant who led them to a dressing room in the back. There the assistant set up a small projector and screen. He placed on a film, activated the projector, and turned down the lights. Galina Rosmanov began to dance. Her fragile body soared through the air, seeming almost weightless as she twisted and turned. It was the first time Saul had seen her in anything except the predeparture record film, and he was totally captivated by her pixieish charm. She wore black leotards. Her hair, pulled into a wide bun, curled around her head like a halo. She had small but well-proportioned breasts and extremely fine legs. "Looks pretty good to me," Saul whispered to Michelle, making it quite clear he wasn't referring to her style of dancing.

"I'm not surprised. You always were attracted to the athletic type. Girls in jogging suits covered with a thin layer of sweat."

"You including yourself in that category?"

"Most assuredly not. I'm too much of a class act to sweat." She grinned. "You should know that. I *perspire,* and even that only in socially acceptable circumstances—poolside at the Cairo Hilton or on the beach on the Costa del Sol."

The film ended. Saul and Michelle left the office and sought out the ballerina who had taken Galina's place.

Her name was Felice Pierenska, and she managed to impart even the most ordinary of movements, drinking water, scratching her arm, closing her eyes, with an incredible grace.

"Tell us about Galina Rosmanov," Saul said to her. "Does she have any enemies?"

"Enemies? Of course. Hundreds." Felice made it sound like the most normal situation in life. "She is a star. She has many enemies. People who envy her talent and her position."

"And you. What about you? What do you think about her?"

"Oh, I despise her." All the while she talked, Felice worked out on the bar, stretching her thighs and her legs, extending her arms. She seemed physically incapable of simply standing still. "I am as good now as Galina ever was, and yet because of her I was continually relegated to a background role. Frankly, I'm glad she's gone, and I hope she never comes back." In a world where only the tough survive, this girl could wind up awfully lonely.

"Can you name anybody she might be close to? Someone she may have confided in?"

Felice peered wickedly out from under half-closed eyelids. She had the devious nature of an adult, but had not yet mastered the aplomb necessary to conceal it. "She has a lover." A tidbit of information she had kept stockpiled in her offensive arsenal for quite some time against just such an eventuality as this. "She keeps him in an apartment in Madrid." Spain was another favorite hangout for Russia's social elite.

"Is he a hydroelectronic engineer by any chance?" asked Saul remembering the notebook.

"No, I believe he is a poet. An *unpublished* poet." Did this girl ever let up?

"Can you give me his address?"

"No, but since Galina distributed her time equally between there and her place in Rome, I would suspect she left it with our tour co-ordinator."

Popovich signaled the resumption of rehearsal, and Felice glided off to center stage, moving her body fluidly, in the prescribed manner, according to official state policy.

No doubt about it. A dancer destined for stardom.

CHAPTER 9

"Remember?" Saul asked as they rode past City Hall on their way into the city from the Madrid terminal. The square behind housed a fine, intimate restaurant called Mesón de San Javier, a place where gourmets savored the roast lamb, and lovers devoured the atmosphere. It had been one of their favorite dining spots during the early, happy part of their marriage. They had bridged there for dinner at least once a month.

"I haven't been to Madrid since," confessed Saul.

Michelle hadn't either, but refused to give Saul whatever slight satisfaction he might derive out of knowing it. In matters concerning money, power, or emotional warmth, she adhered to the principle of the one-way trade. Take but never give. She spent the remainder of their journey staring out the window in silence, watching without visible reaction as bittersweet memory after bittersweet memory passed her by.

The cab pulled up outside an upper-class apartment building. A tattered Russian flag hung limp and lifeless outside, as though after years of trying, the wind had finally beaten it into submission.

On the building's directory Saul checked the apartment number the Kirov's tour co-ordinator had given as Galina's. The number listed two names. G. Rosmanov and someone name Kurchienka, no first initial.

Saul knocked on the door.

"Yes, who is it," answered a high, artificially girlish voice.

"My name is Saul Lukas. I work for the American Bridge Authority. I'm investigating the disappearance of Galina Rosmanov."

"Oh yes. Of course." A slim boy, barely into his twenties,

opened the door. He was a Negro, his skin the color of butter and honey, with almond-shaped, faintly oriental eyes. He wore a bulky fisherman's knit sweater over black leotards and sported lip gloss, eye shadow, and blusher. His outfit and makeup would have been considered extremely stylish on a man in any other country in the world. But not in Russia, nor, by ideological extension, here in Spain. Here such affectations were still the exclusive hallmark of the homosexual, hardly the type of companion Saul would have expected to find being kept by an attractive, and distinctly feminine, worldwide celebrity.

The boy stood aside so they could enter. The interior of the apartment gave Saul a strong sense of déjà vu, since it almost precisely duplicated Galina's other apartment. The same colors, the same furniture, the same area rugs. But this one didn't have quite the same casual elegance. The picture groupings were improperly balanced, the furniture badly placed, as though Galina had hired a professional decorator to do her apartment in Rome and had then frugally attempted to adapt the design herself for use here.

"My name is Kurchienka," said Galina's roommate, "but everyone calls me Kurch."

Old stereotypes die hard. Saul was greatly surprised by the strength of Kurchienka's handshake. "This is Michelle Warren," he said, "the Bridge Authority's director."

"Charmed." Kurch extended his hand to Michelle, backside up, as though he expected her to kiss it.

Michelle pulled it down, shook it briefly, and released it, treating it roughly the same way she would a two-week dead fish.

"You said you're investigating Galina's disappearance," said Kurchienka. "Have you made any headway?"

"Yes," said Saul, "we think we've found her, but we have no idea whether or not she's alive."

"Oh, God!" Kurchienka slumped into an easy chair, thrust his head backward against the cushion and moaned, rather theatrically, as if he had learned to demonstrate grief by aping actresses in old Hollywood movies. "I suspected something dreadful was going to happen to her. She's been acting so strangely lately. Do you have a hanky I could borrow?" he asked Saul.

Saul tugged his handkerchief out of his back pocket and handed it to Kurchienka. "You say she's been acting strangely. In what way?"

Kurchienka dabbed at his eyes, but delicately so as not to accidentally dislodge one of his false eyelashes. "Well, she became increasingly involved in this fantasy of hers. She talked constantly of amassing enough money to retire and live in great splendor on top of a high mountain." He passed the handkerchief back, hanging onto it for just a second longer than he had to after Saul took the other end. "It's also ironic that she should disappear inside a bridge."

"How so?" Saul took a seat across from him.

Kurchienka flicked his eyes at Michelle, slanted forward, and dropped his voice, making it quite plain his confidences were intended for Saul alone. "Well, for the past few months, she's been obsessed with bridges. She bought route maps. Read technical manuals on matter transference. She rambled on incessantly about how convenient it would be to have her own personal bridge so she could come and go at will. Bridges came to fascinate her."

"Any idea why?"

"God only knows. She was never interested in such things before. I told her several times that I found this new infatuation of hers to be a silly bore, but of course she ignored me." He placed his hand casually on Saul's knee. "We never had a real relationship, if you understand me. I was never more to her than a plaything, a replacement when she grew too old for dolls."

"Was she taking drugs of any sort?"

"Of course." Kurchienka spread his hands and shook them like an old-time minstrel singer. "Everyone takes drugs."

"I found a vial of tablets and some powder in her other apartment. Any idea what they might be?"

"The powder could have been cocaine. Galina routinely smuggled it back with her every time she went to Mexico. But the tablets? She never took tablets. She said they upset her stomach. The only drugs I ever saw her take in tablet form were an occasional aspirin, her birth control tablets, and of course that tablet you take before you ride the wires."

Michelle walked around behind Saul's chair, put her hands on his shoulders, and leaned slightly across him, so Kurchienka could not address Saul without addressing her as well. "Do you know of any reason why anyone would want to harm Galina?" she asked.

"Harm her? Harm Galina?" Kurchienka giggled and threw back his head like a mare in heat. "What a foolish question. I don't know of anyone who *wouldn't* want to harm Galina. She took married men for lovers, persuaded them to abandon their families, and then dropped them. She conducted vicious whispering campaigns against her rivals at the Kirov. I honestly wouldn't have been surprised to hear that she kicked dogs and stole candy from children. An absolutely perfect bitch."

"Yet she couldn't have been totally without redeeming qualities," Michelle pointed out. "You, for instance, obviously found her tolerable."

Kurchienka denied this with the same fervor an accused maniac would protest innocence of an ax murder. "Quite to the contrary. She abused me terribly." He grabbed onto the back of Saul's hand. "She called me rotten names. Threatened to turn me over to the authorities because of my . . . sexual preferences."

"Why didn't you leave her then?" asked Michelle.

"You have to understand my position," said Kurchienka, extending his head upward toward her like a penitent sinner reaching for a communion wafer. "I'm a poet. It's very important for a poet to have a reservoir of suffering which can be translated into verse. Galina provided me with an exposure to pain."

"Pounding yourself over the head with a hammer would have fulfilled your apprenticeship even faster," said Michelle but loudly enough so only Saul could hear.

"Did Galina have many lovers?" asked Saul.

Kurchienka spent an unreasonably long time contemplating his answer, as if he couldn't quite determine how to interpret such a question. "She had men who loved her," he said finally, "but she didn't love any of them back. I suppose in the final analysis she loved only herself."

"Who were some of these men?" asked Michelle. "Do you know their names?"

"No. Only that they were very important. She used to brag

about them. Highly placed Russian and Chinese diplomats. American athletes. Israeli scientists."

"Scientists, you say." Saul pursued his one slim lead. "Anyone involved in hydroelectronic engineering?"

"I rather doubt it." Kurchienka fussed with a ball of lint caught on the front of his sweater. "That wouldn't have half enough glamour for Galina. She leaned more toward nuclear physicists or neurosurgeons. Lately, for instance, she had been seeing a matter transference expert. I think that's what got her started on her whole captivation with bridges. But no hydroelectronic engineers, no, no one like that."

"What about the diplomats? Did she ever tell you their names?"

"No."

"Did she ever tell you the names of any of her men?"

"No."

"Did she ever insinuate that anyone might be revealing classified information to her?"

"No."

"Did Galina ever contemplate marriage?" asked Michelle.

Kurchienka gave out with the kind of shrill cackle more likely heard in a barnyard. "To Galina, claustrophobia wasn't a small, dark closet. It was a permanent relationship." His dramatic phrasing and practiced delivery led Saul to suspect he had used that line more than once before.

"There was a rumor she was about to defect to the United States. Any truth to it?"

Kurchienka ran his hands down first one leg and then the other, like a marathon runner trying to rid himself of cramps midway through an especially grueling race. "I don't know. But if she was, I would say it was your country, not mine that would have been most anxious to prevent it."

"Could you explain that?" said Michelle, clearly puzzled by such a paradoxical statement.

"Lately Galina had become a great liability to my government, always talking out against the stifling of free expression the way she did. Her actions certainly would not have gone unpunished had she not been of such international prominence. I believe my government would have been delighted to be rid of her. Your country, on the other hand, is currently engaged in rather sensitive talks with mine on the subject of mutually limiting the spread of the military bridge networks. Her defection at this point could have proven extremely embarrassing."

After another half hour of essentially unproductive questioning, they thanked Kurchienka for his trouble and left. Saul had to do quite a fast shuffle to avoid being kissed good-by at the door.

"I thought for a minute there you were going to ask him to go steady," said Michelle while they waited for their cab.

"Jealous?" Saul responded flatly.

Oddly enough, she was, but, luckily for her, the cab pulled up and she was able to climb inside before Saul had a chance to read it in her face.

When they returned to Mexico City, Ralph Ferguson awaited them in recovery. "I think you'd both best get ready for another trip," he told them the instant they came around. "Galina Rosmanov just popped out of the wires."

CHAPTER 10

Two hours later Saul and Michelle were in Switzerland speeding up a mountain road in the back seat of a white Mercedes limousine. Discreet gold letters spelled out Ryker Sanitarium on the limo's left hand door. Saul had never been to the sanitarium before, had not even been aware of its existence until Michelle revealed it to him almost as an afterthought on their way to Zurich predeparture.

"The Bridge Authority maintains this . . . this sort of combination hospital/hotel," Michelle had said. "In the Swiss Alps. About thirty kilometers north of Zurich. A very nice facility, quite pleasant, with a beautiful view. Patients there eat the finest food, drink the finest wines, see the latest movies."

"Sounds great," said Saul. "I'd like to recuperate there myself. How sick do I have to be to get in?"

"Very." No matter how she phrased it, her explication was bound to imbue her with the shattered credibility of a trusted employee caught with both arms sunk to the elbow in the company cashbox, so she gave it to Saul straight and unfrosted, in the simplest possible terms. "We run Ryker to house travelers who pop out of the wires misaligned."

Their hostess began her standard predeparture spiel, but Saul, who had heard it so many times he could recite it by heart, waved her off. "You can't be serious. That kind of accident can't happen. It's physically impossible."

The hostess returned with two recovery tablets. Michelle took both, swallowed one and passed the other to Saul. "No, it's not."

He took the tablet she gave him and kneaded it between his fingers, as if trying to buff it free of contaminants left there by her touch. "You'd better have one hell of a reason for suppressing a fact like that."

Michelle passed through weigh-in, and entered isolation. Saul did the same. They continued to communicate through intercoms. "You'll understand when we arrive. Those people are human beings only in the broadest sense of the term. Absolutely horrible things have happened to them. Ghastly things I hate to even think about. Organs materialized outside the body. Legs and arms transposed. Parts of the skeletal system distorted."

"What do you tell their families?"

"That they've been lost in the wires. Our on-staff psychologists tell us that's best. It would be devastating for next of kin to see a loved one in a misaligned state."

"Not to mention the effect on your profit picture if word ever got out."

"That's unfair, Saul. Some misalignments require fantastically complex life-support systems. We've spent fortunes developing, constructing, and maintaining them. We also see to it that next of kin receive a most generous lifetime annuity to compensate them for their loss."

Saul looked at the transportal. He had never realized until just that instant the resemblance between it and an upended coffin. "My God. To think I used to laugh at Herman for not riding wire. When it turns out he was perfectly correct. This stuff about accident-free travel is a total fabrication."

"No, it's not that bad." She opened her purse, poked about inside, and pulled out a tube of lipstick. Her lips had suddenly become very dry, the way they did when she negotiated contracts with a weak union, fired an incompetent aide, or signed a layoff order. When she knew she bargained from a strength no one could possibly overcome. "It happens to less than point-zero-zero-zero-four per cent of all travelers." Michelle spit out statistics the way steel mills poured forth ingots, with enough red-hot insistency behind them to incinerate anything in their path. "Taken on a statistical basis, that's almost no chance at all."

Unconsciously, Saul rubbed his exercise-toughened abdominal muscles, trying to imagine what it would feel like to have his stomach suddenly turned inside out. "Why wasn't I ever told about this?"

"Since the matter doesn't fall within your bailiwick, I didn't feel it necessary."

"How many people do you have secreted at this hideaway of yours?"

"It varies. As you might imagine, misalignments tend to have very short lifetimes. I believe the current population to be somewhere in the vicinity of two hundred."

The limousine rounded a bend, and Saul got his first glimpse of Ryker Sanitarium. The complex consisted of forty rectangular white buildings, laid out nearly end to end like a concrete bandage overlaying a narrow strip of wounded flatland gouged out of the side of the mountain. A ten-foot-high chain-link fence surrounded the area. Pine trees planted at regular intervals along the fence did little to alter the sanitarium's distinct resemblance to a medium-security prison.

The guard at the main gate recognized Michelle instantly and waved the limo through with a brisk salute.

The limo pulled up outside a building labeled "Administration." Michelle led Saul through an outer waiting room, into the office behind. There she introduced him to Dr. Warner Ryker who, with his short, rotund build, white hair, and long white beard, bore an amazing resemblance to Santa Claus.

"Ralph Ferguson told us you have Galina Rosmanov here," said Saul.

"Yes, yes." Ryker's head bobbed agreeably, a furry basketball bouncing downcourt toward the final, game-ending goal. "Ralph made the identification personally via closed-circuit TV. She popped out of a terminal in Albuquerque, about two hours ago."

"May I see her?" Saul asked.

Ryker stroked his fingers gingerly through his beard, as though afraid of what he might encounter nesting within. "Have you ever seen a misalignment before?"

"No, never."

"Then I must first caution you. Misalignments bear strong resemblances to horror-movie monsters. It's very difficult for an untrained observer to retain a suitably detached air."

Saul flashed on a vision of the Creature from the Black Lagoon *en pointe* in *tutu* and ballet slippers, but quickly blanked it from his mind. "I'll do my best."

"Fine, fine." Ryker led Saul and Michelle to the door. "Shall we go?"

In a small golf cart they threaded through the complex to one of the outlying buildings. Inside, armed guards stood at the front of each of the eight doors opening onto the central corridor. "Our newcomers' facility," Ryker explained. "We find it best to keep them under lock and key until they adjust to their new format. After six weeks or so they are transferred to one of the permanent residents' wings. There they are given their own rooms and allowed to roam about more or less on their own."

"So long as they don't leave the complex," said Saul.

"Oh, heavens no. Naturally we can't permit that," Ryker answered. "Rosmanov, Rosmanov." Ryker read the typewritten nametags stuck to each door. "Rosmanov. Yes, here we are. Galina Rosmanov. You can see her in there. Through the window."

Saul took a look. The pathetic piece of humanity huddling on the floor of the furnitureless padded cell bore absolutely no resemblance whatsoever to the graceful ballerina Saul had seen dancing in the film in Washington. For starters, this person had no head. Her eyes, nose, and mouth protruded from a gruesome bump in the center of her back. She had only one arm and no feet. She reminded Saul of the babies displayed in courtrooms during the trials of careless drug companies or depraved Nazi scientists. "How can you be sure this is Galina Rosmanov?"

"We do a thorough cross-check," said Ryker. "We find out who is missing, compare their molecular I.D. patterns to the misaligned, and, if we get a match, well, we get a match."

"So, on the basis of your cross-check, you concluded that the girl in there, who must be, or must have been, nearly six feet tall and must have weighed nearly 150 pounds is Galina Rosmanov."

Ryker moved his mouth, but no sounds came out. Quickly, Michelle rushed to his aid. "You have to remember, Saul," she said, "that misalignment can do strange things to a person's physiology. Elongate the body cavity, foreshorten the extremities. We see it all the time. Isn't that right, Dr. Ryker."

Ryker mopped a monogrammed silk handkerchief across the

bubbles of dampness that had suddenly surfaced on his forehead. "Yes, yes, happens quite often. Can't tell one from the other by just looking at them. Have to study the molecular patterns. Really the only way to be sure."

Never had Saul seen such a bad liar. Ryker nearly choked on the tangle of loose ends constituting his falsehood. With a face as transparent as that, Saul hoped for Ryker's own sake the man never took up poker. He'd lose his stethoscope. Saul turned in disgust and walked out of the building.

"That wasn't Galina Rosmanov, and you know it," Saul told Michelle on their way down the mountain. "You trotted out some unrecognizable specimen, slapped a phony nametag on her, and tried to pass her off. True?"

Michelle thumped her fist against her armrest.

Saul grabbed Michelle by the elbow and turned her to face him. "Why?"

Michelle shook loose of his grip, scrunched down into her seat, and leaned her head back so far she stared straight up at the roof. "You wouldn't understand, Saul. There's more to it than one missing girl. Much, much more. The future of civilization."

The ridiculous implications of such an assertion almost caused Saul to laugh out loud. "Now that's good. Galina Rosmanov. Ninety-eight pound toe dancer. Cornerstone of a plot to topple democracy. That's good, Michelle, really good."

"I didn't say democracy, Saul." Michelle sat upright, turned and looked him straight in the eyes, her voice level and unemotional, as though she were doing no more than reading him the sunrise schedules from next year's almanac. "I said civilization. Ours, hers, everyone's. For once trust me, Saul. Leave her in the wires. Believe me, she's better off forgotten."

She slumped back against the seat and obstinately refused to say more.

They detoured through New York City so Saul could visit the Bridge Authority's drug lab and pick up their analysis of the tablets and the powder he had found in Galina's apartment.

"Nothing so far on the powder," said the scientist who had run the scan. "But those tablets! A blend of synthetics. Closely akin to the drug taken before riding the wires."

At that Michelle, who had been pacing impatiently from one side of the lab to the other stopped and stared at him.

"In the same generic family," the scientist went on, "but ever so slightly different. I ran some tests and, believe it or not, when I gave it to a lab animal and transported it, the animal recovered instantly. No time lag involved whatsoever. I propose we do further testing. If this stuff proves out, it portends a radical breakthrough in transference state of the art. May I ask where you got it?"

Saul put the remaining tablets into their vial and stuffed them into his pocket. "Let's just say I stumbled onto it."

Michelle halted him the moment they were outside. "Give me the tablets, Saul."

"Why should I?"

"Because they belong to the Bridge Authority. They were stolen from us." Her hand, which she held palm up, curled into a fist, then just as quickly unclenched, as if she couldn't quite decide whether to beg or demand.

Saul pulled out the vial and tossed it into the air, catching it quickly and closing his hand over it when she made a grab in its direction. "You mean to tell me you've known about this drug all along and haven't made it public?"

"That's right. We've had it for years. We've never merchandised it because of the economics involved. It takes a great deal of power to keep a bridge operating. That power is a constant factor, it's the same no matter what the length of the trip. We can't run bridges economically if there are more short runs than long. If the existence of this drug ever became public knowledge, it would put great pressure on us to set up coast-to-coast or even worldwide networks of short-haul bridges. Such a move would cut greatly into our profits."

"So Galina Rosmanov stays in the wires and the Bridge Authority stays in the black."

"That's part of it, yes. There's more, but that's enough." Michelle pulled out her checkbook, placed it against a building, and began to write. "Here, Saul," she said as she scribbled her signature. "A bonus. Take a vacation. Forget about Galina Rosmanov. She's just a small piece in a total picture you're not equipped to see."

When she turned to hand Saul the check, he was gone.

CHAPTER 11

Saul, Herman, and Rosie sat around a circular table in the collector station cafeteria. The table had been pushed against a wall to clear enough space for twenty-five folding cots; the station's normal crew of thirty had been expanded nearly sevenfold by the personnel—engineers, mathematicians, technicians—involved in the effort to extricate Galina Rosmanov.

"I can't figure it," Saul said, pouring himself another cup of coffee from the pot plugged into the tabletop warmer. "The Bridge Authority doesn't want Galina out. The Russians don't want her out. But what could she possibly have done to become such a threat to powers like that?" Even though he drank his coffee unsweetened, Saul still gave it a ritual stir, a habit leftover from his younger days, when two lumps of sugar had added to his energy instead of to the bulge around his middle. "Herman, how long can she last in there?"

Herman, stooped over the table, his coffee mug gripped in both hands, didn't respond. He stared, preoccupied, off into space, lost in his thoughts.

Gently, Saul shook his shoulder. "Herman, how much longer can we expect to hold Galina Rosmanov in the collector before she starts to dissipate?"

Herman blinked rapidly a few times, as though Saul had awakened him from a deep sleep and he had to reaccustom his eyes to the light. "Beg pardon?"

Saul repeated his question for the third time. "How much longer can Galina Rosmanov hang on in the collector before she starts to dissipate?"

Herman spun his mug in a circle about its own axis and watched it gradually wind down like a dying world trapped atop a galaxy of solid Formica. "I don't know, Saul. I honestly don't know. She could last for a day or two, she could go within an hour. I simply don't know."

"Have you made any progress toward freeing her?"

"None." Herman picked up his mug and took a drink, needing both hands to guide it to his mouth.

"What can I do?" asked Saul.

"Well, if I knew how much her weight had been altered, that would help some."

"And if you did know, what are the odds you could get her out. Fifty per cent? Forty?"

Herman poured himself a refill, again needing both hands to hold the pot steady. "No, not that good. I would say five to ten per cent. That's just a guess, though. It could be lower."

Saul shook his head. "You're certainly no fountain of good cheer, Herman."

"It's in the numbers, Saul." Herman reached into his shirt pocket and pulled out his hand calculator. "I tell you what the numbers tell me. I can't change the numbers."

"And how about you, Rosie? Any impressions?"

Rosie had taken only one short nap in the previous forty-eight hours, yet it didn't seem to have had any visible effect on her. It was as if she were drawing her strength from some hidden reservoir unavailable to anyone else. "I get a fleeting vision, Saul. A terrific flush of freedom. A floating sensation. Somewhat akin to rapture of the deep. Saul, from what I'm picking up, Galina Rosmanov is gloriously happy inside the wire. She doesn't want to come out. Not ever."

"Oh, that's just great. That makes it unanimous. Michelle stops just short of ordering me to pack up and go home. You, Rosie, tell me the girl's happy where she's at. And Herman, according to you, we don't stand the chance of a snowball in hell of shaking her loose anyway. Well, I've got a surprise for everybody. I'm paid to get people out of the wires. Whether they want to come out or not. Whether it's politically advantageous for them to come out or not. Whether the numbers say they'll come out or not. I get them out. That's my job, and I do it. Without exception."

Saul noticed that Herman, once again, had drifted off into a meditative reverie and appeared not to have heard a word he had said. "Herman, you feel all right?"

Herman spoke strangely, as though his mouth had developed a rictus and could no longer manage the precise movements needed to form words. "I don't know, Saul. I've got this tingling sensation throughout my body."

"Can you make it? You want me to scout up a replacement?" They both knew that to be impossible. Herman was unique in his knowledge of matter transference. He had no replacement.

"No. I'll be all right. I think it's just poor circulation. I'll be fine."

Before Saul could voice any further concern, Herman rose from the table and headed off in the direction of the main computer.

"Where do we go from here?" asked Rosie.

"I don't know. I guess I try and find out how Galina's weight was altered, and by how much. To do that, I check everybody who might have wanted her croaked. And it looks like that just might comprise the world's least exclusive club."

"She was not a well-loved person?"

"Hardly. Her fellow dancers hated her. She broke up more marriages than all the lawyers in Tijuana. She stole top-secret drugs from the Bridge Authority. A multifaceted girl."

Rosie chuckled. "Sounds like just your type."

The corners of Saul's mouth turned upward into the faintest trace of a smile. "Maybe that's why I'm so anxious to get her out. Anybody working that many angles has just got to be able to teach me something."

"Mr. Lukas," said Saul's secretary threading her way through the maze of cots. "You have a call from Mexico City."

"Right there," Saul said. He walked to the nearest wallphone, punched the flashing button, and picked up the handset. "Saul Lukas," he said.

"I have information about Galina Rosmanov," croaked a muffled, obviously disguised female voice. "If you want to hear it, be at the northeast gate of the Plaza del Toros in Mexico City in two hours. Be on time, and be alone."

"What kind of information? And who are you?"

"Be on time, and be alone."

The phone buzzed in his hand as the caller broke the connection.

Saul waited at the northeast gate of the Plaza del Toros. Fifteen minutes. Thirty. Forty-five. Nobody came. He decided to give it another quarter hour and then chalk off the entire affair as a hoax. His arbitrary time limit had nearly expired when a small beggar girl approached him and held out her hand.

As Saul reached into his pocket for change, a strong pair of arms encircled him from the rear. Another pair of arms covered his mouth and nose with a chemical-drenched rag. Saul tried to shake loose, but the harder he struggled, the weaker he became. He made one final ineffectual effort to free himself, and then passed into unconsciousness.

He awakened roped tightly to a chair inside a darkened, thoroughly soundproofed room. Not a trace of light or noise leaked in from outside to give him the slightest hint as to where he was. A very professional touch.

"Good evening, Mr. Lukas." A woman came around in front of him and flipped on a tiny pinlight suspended between them. Saul recognized her instantly. Mary Hemke. Leader of One World United, a group advocating the abolition of national boundaries and the formation of a single world government. With OWU at the head, of course. Since nobody with a cause was content to just ask nicely anymore, the OWU underscored their demands for support by kidnapping prominent businessmen, executing government officials, exploding bombs in corporate headquarters, and robbing banks. As a result Mary Hemke was wanted by nearly every country in the world.

"Mary Hemke, isn't it?"

"I see I've gained international renown." She sat down across from Saul and gracefully crossed her legs at the knee.

"Become notorious I think would be a better choice of words." Try as hard as he might, Saul couldn't conceive of this woman as a dangerous urban guerrilla. No jungle fatigues, sling-held submachine gun, combat boots, hair full of twigs or wild rhetoric here. Mary was smartly groomed, extremely attractive, and pleasantly soft-spoken. Her blond hair fell to her shoulders in bubbly swirls that brushed across her cheeks like wisps of silk dipped in sunshine. Her smile would have done credit to a toothpaste commercial. Of course, what better place to hide a razor-sharp bayonet than inside an angel cake frosted with spun-sugar rosebuds? "I assume it was you I spoke to on the phone."

"Correct."

"You said you had information about Galina Rosmanov."

Mary locked her intertwined hands around her legs and nodded. "Galina Rosmanov was one of us."

"She was in the OWU?"

"Not as an operational participant, no, but in spirit, yes. She came to us about six months ago with an incredible story. She said she would sell us an item which would help our cause immeasurably."

"A Russian hydrogen bomb?" Saul heard feet shuffling uneasily behind him and was overcome by the queasy realization that his joke might not be so farfetched.

"Hardly." Mary pointed a finger at Saul. The gesture carried a strong hint of hostility, to be expected since Mary had a clear-cut method of segmenting humanity. Friends on one side, enemies on the other. And, since Saul had not yet proved himself her friend, that left only one category remaining. "A wireless bridge, Mr. Lukas, a wireless bridge." Her voice echoed another, which, in earlier days, had persuaded millions of normally sane people to goose-step a thousand leagues across the world. "Think of it. With such a device, we could set up transportals anyplace. Traditional national boundaries would disintegrate. We would become, finally, one unified world. If you want to go somewhere, you go there. Without having to factor yourself through a complex system of petty bureaucrats, first."

A wireless bridge? It seemed impossible, but then, less than 160 years earlier, so had radio and television. "Surely you didn't believe her?"

"Not at first. To counter my skepticism, she showed me an eight-millimeter movie of her device in action. And it worked, Mr. Lukas, it worked."

"Trick photography?"

"No. Our film experts, the ones who do our informational documentaries, checked it out very carefully. No question about it. What she showed us was actually a film of a crude, but fully operational wireless bridge."

"Where did she get such a thing?"

"She refused to say."

"You still have that movie?"

"No. She wouldn't let it out of her possession."

"What was her price?"

Mary leaned back in her chair and tossed out the figure slowly, unreeling it zero by zero. "Ten million dollars."

Saul wondered how many banks the OWU had to rob to pull together a nest egg that size. "And you were going to buy?"

"She was to have delivered it to us prior to her performance at the Kennedy Center. It's my belief she probably had it with her when she disappeared."

"She was carrying a wireless bridge in her luggage? It's that small?"

"Judging from the one demonstrated in the movie, no more than one foot by three feet by three feet." She showed him the unit's size by spacing apart her hands. If her estimate was accurate, the unit was compact enough to fit easily into the footlocker Galina had carried into the wires with her.

"The inventor of this wireless bridge. You ever meet him? She ever mention his name?"

"No never. We dealt only with her."

"That's not much to go on."

"It wasn't my intention to give you clues, Mr. Lukas, but rather to convey a message. We're prepared to pay ten million dollars for that wireless bridge. To whoever delivers it to us."

"Great. In the meantime, could you advance me five pesos for busfare home."

He felt the chemical rag encircle his mouth and nose, and once again he passed into a deep, dreamless sleep.

CHAPTER 12

Saul and Herman entered the lounge adjacent to the collector station's computer room. They found Herman's girlfriend there, fast asleep on a sofa. She had covered herself with one of the twenty-gallon red-canvas sacks the station's programmers used to cart away discarded punched paper tape. The Bridge Authority's name and logo, stenciled across the sack's middle, rose and fell in time to her breathing. Herman lifted her head and slid wearily under it, making her a pillow with his lap. Saul grabbed a chair, a large overstuffed recliner, and wrestled it to Herman's end of the sofa.

"What's up?" Herman asked when they were both seated.

"I've got a hypothetical question."

Herman surfed his hand through the ripples in the sleeping girl's hair. "To that kind I give hypothetical answers."

"Understood. Here's my question." As the words rolled off his tongue, Saul experienced the fluttery mixture of fear and fascination that must have gripped ancient mariners as they approached what their maps told them to be the edge of the world. "Given current matter transference technology, is it feasible that anyone could build a wireless bridge?"

Herman's eyes glazed over momentarily, then rebounded, but only to a level of intensity just about equal to the gloomy washed-out luminescence of auto headlights in the cortege of a daylight funeral. "This is only because you and I go back a long way together, and it's strictly between you, me, and the walls."

Herman's uncharacteristic solemnity was more than enough to convince Saul he wasn't going to like what he was about to hear. "Absolutely confidential, old buddy."

Herman leaned close to Saul, as though his words were ponderously heavy and might sink to the floor unless he cut down the distance they had to traverse. "We finished the first wireless link nearly a year ago. I'd been working on it exclusively for almost a year prior to that."

So, something else that apparently did not fall within Saul's bailiwick. He wondered how many more surprises would come crawling out from under the rocks before this affair was over.

"It was a hush-hush, top secret, joint Army/Bridge Authority operation." Perhaps by accident, perhaps by design, Herman's hand covered the sleeping girl's ear. "It's still highly classified. One of those sole-source, fixed-fee-plus-expenses deals Congress gets so upset about. The Bridge Authority got a guaranteed half billion for the installation of a link between Washington and L.A. That price, by the way, didn't include the fixed-position satellite we had to put in orbit as a signal bounce—the wireless system is strictly line of sight. Later the Army renegotiated, upped the profit a billion in return for which we added another satellite and a third portal in Germany."

"Those are pretty large sums of money you're flinging around. Regular transportals go for only a fraction of that. Why the big bucks here?"

"Several reasons. While we can crank out a wire transportal in two weeks max, we can't turn out a wireless in less than ten months. Quality-control checks alone eat up six to eight weeks. And the raw materials. It would boggle your mind to know how much metal goes into one of those things."

That, taken together with what Mary Hemke had told him, struck a distinctly jarring note. "How much metal can something that small use?"

"Small?" Herman's chuckle metamorphosed into a dense, bronchial cough. "Small, you say? Maybe if you're Paul Bunyon. Saul, those three wireless bridges are each the size of a missile silo. They weigh hundreds of thousands of tons. Their shielding alone is four feet of solid lead. The focusing mechanism would dwarf this entire station."

"That must be the giant economy version. For zapping whole battalions back and forth."

"Hardly. The transference capacity of a wireless bridge is less than twenty-five kilos." He checked out the room but saw nothing of equivalent size to use as a visual aid. "The reason capacity is so relatively low is because there's an inverse logarithmic relationship between transfer weight and power, an effect far greater than the one we work with on wire. It has to do with preventing scatter and maintaining cohesion. It wasn't just a matter of changing a few dials around and hauling up the wires. This isn't just a refinement of the net as we know it. It's so far beyond anything we've ever done before, that it might as well be an entirely new technique."

"What about prototype models?"

"We prototyped on the computer. The first working version, the one in Washington, went up full scale. It performed flawlessly from day one, and has continued to do so ever since."

"You never did anything littler? Say small enough to fit inside a steamer trunk?"

Herman obviously found that statement uproariously funny, but his deteriorating physical condition left him without enough surplus strength to squander on something as nonessential to life support as a belly laugh. "Steamer trunk? Lord, no. I wish we had achieved that kind of miniaturization. We're years away from anything so tiny. We can only take our power-to-shielding ratio to certain fixed limits before we experience dangerous side effects, radiation leakage, overheating, beam scatter, that kind of stuff. Of course, if we get a breakthrough in metallurgy or high-energy physics, we might be able to put together a more compact unit, say one the size of a boxcar or a small house. But we're still years away from even that."

"What about the Russians? Or the Israelis? Either one of them have the ability to construct a fully portable wireless bridge?"

Herman started to shake his head even before Saul had completely finished. "Hardly. They've got their hands full keeping their *wire* networks on-line. And a wireless net is a thousand times more complex. No, neither one of them could do it."

"One last question. Could someone use one of these wireless bridges to transport something into the wires?"

"No. Impossible." Herman extended his hands, palms up, as though he held an example of both networks, one in each hand. His right hand was considerably higher than his left. "The two systems aren't compatible. They're both exclusively point to point, sender to receiver. They couldn't possibly interface. There's no way whatsoever for something like that to happen." He dropped his hands. So far, Saul had asked all the questions. Now it was Herman's turn. "Incidentally, why the sudden interest in wireless bridges?"

Saul rubbed the back of his neck in an effort to untangle the coil of tension wrapped around the channel to his brain. "I got a tip that Galina Rosmanov was carrying a wireless bridge in her luggage."

Herman slapped the sofa's arm. "That's funny. In her luggage, you say? My God, the overweight charges would have bankrupted Saudi Arabia. In her luggage? That's good. Obviously the bridge wasn't one of ours."

"Hardly. According to my source, this bridge measured approximately one foot by three by three."

The edges of Herman's mouth dripped down into the kind of contemplative scowl one might expect to see on the face of a veteran umpire who had just been shown conclusive proof he had botched his call of a crucial play. "That's pretty small. Your source ever actually see it operate?"

"No, not in person. They saw movies, though."

"Film can be hyped."

"They say they checked and found no evidence of it."

Herman leaned back in the sofa and smiled, his confidence in his scientific prowess restored. "Then I'd say they were wrong. Given a choice between that movie being a phony and Galina Rosmanov having a suitcase-sized wireless bridge, there's only one logical choice."

Saul stood up. "That's what I suspected. Still, the story had just enough ring of truth about it to make me want to pursue it further."

Herman caught Saul by the arm and pulled him closer. "Tell you what," he whispered. "If and when you ever do come up with a wireless bridge that size, I sure would appreciate getting first look-see." He winked broadly.

"Sure," said Saul. "Can you top ten million dollars?"

"Beg pardon?"

"Nothing. A bad joke." He patted Herman's hand. "I'll be in Mexico City. Let me know if anything develops."

After Saul left, Herman tried to get up, but couldn't. His legs would not respond. He struggled so hard to stand, that he awoke the sleeping girl.

With her help he finally managed to get to his feet only to find he had also lost the ability to walk. Leaning on her shoulder, he hobbled to the computer room. There he sat down before the main terminal, placed his hands on the keyboard, and immediately lost interest in the functional ability of anything below his waist.

CHAPTER 13

Saul arrived in Mexico City during the dinner hour. The desk clerk at Michelle's hotel told him she was dining that evening at Caballo Bayo, a country inn that had lately become a great favorite with status-conscious American tourists. Since Saul cared little for status and even less for American tourists, he had never been there.

At the entrance, the inn blew whatever slim shot it might have had at winning his regular trade. The doorman would not let him in without a tie.

Grumbling a condemnation of establishments that contrived atmosphere by enforcing adherence to outmoded standards, Saul went down the street until he came to an all-night market. In the back, between a rack of potato chips and a cooler piled with Carta Blanca hung a display of ties, the majority of them spotted and stained. Saul picked one at random. It was made of shiny rayon, bore a hand-painted picture of a matador, and had obviously seen numerous better evenings. The clerk at the counter, obviously familiar with Caballo Bayo's policy, offered him a rent-or-buy option. He bought, taking great care to obtain an itemized and dated receipt for inclusion in his expense report.

He returned to the inn, made it past the doorman, and asked the maître d' for Michelle.

The maître d' walked up a nearby flight of stairs and knocked discreetly on one of several doors leading off a second-story balcony overlooking the main dining room. The door opened a crack and a head peeked out. Michelle's secretary. He conversed briefly with the maître d', shut the door, opened it a few seconds later and spoke with the maître d' again.

The maître d' returned and told Saul that Miss Warren would

see him momentarily. That moment stretched out to thirty minutes before Michelle finally opened the door and motioned for Saul to come up. When he entered the room, Michelle was alone, her secretary apparently on the other side of a door leading into what Saul assumed was a private bath.

The room was furnished in the style of a nineteenth-century Mexican hacienda. A roughhewn oak table surrounded by six ornately carved chairs. A geometrically patterned wool carpet highlighting the deep texture of adobe walls. Wall sconces and table-top candelabra of solid silver.

A heavy wooden, cowhide-upholstered sofa occupied the entire length of one wall. Saul tested it by pressing it with his hand to determine if it was really as uncomfortable as it looked. "Extra firm," he said to Michelle. "Great for the back."

Michelle pointed at his chest. "Love your tie. Let me guess. Saks? No, not with that Southwestern ethnic flavor. I guess Niemans."

"I think the sign said 'Jose's Fashion Boutique and Cut-Rate Liquor Store.' "

Michelle sat down at the table, which was set for two, and poured herself a glass from a half-empty bottle of champagne. She didn't offer any to Saul. "You've made some progress?"

"In a way. I've stumbled onto a very interesting situation. It seems there's a story going around that Galina Rosmanov was carrying a wireless bridge with her when she entered the wires."

"Impossible. There is no such a thing." Michelle spoke with the certainty of a prophetess who had just descended from a mountaintop where she had received her information direct from the Lord Himself.

"Mercy me." Saul raised his eyebrows in mock surprise. "You mean you haven't heard? Let me be the first to break the news. The Bridge Authority has thus far built *three* wireless bridges. Taking them from west to east around the world, they're in Los Angeles, Washington, and Germany. I'm sorry I can't be more specific about the German location, but I'm sure with your contacts in the business you can dredge it out of somebody."

Nonplussed, Michelle switched stories with the slightly haughty ease of a wine steward replacing a rejected vintage. "That's top-secret information, Saul. I don't know where you got it, and I don't want to. Just understand that disclosure could set our national defense posture back years."

"Hey, I'm the original all-American boy. I wear red, white, and blue jockey shorts. My country, right or wrong. So how about leveling with me? What's the story on these wireless bridges?"

Michelle didn't seem unduly perturbed at Saul's knowledge. She acted more like someone esconced in a storm cellar, secure in the realization her fortifications were more than ample safely to weather the tornado swirling around her. "About five years ago the government approached us with a plan for a crash program aimed at developing a wireless military bridge network. At the time, no one in the Bridge Authority, not even your friend Lindstrom, thought such a net could be built, but the money was good, so we took the commission anyway."

"That's the spirit that's made America great."

She pointedly ignored his sarcasm. "To summarize, we got lucky, Lindstrom and some of our organic researchers came through, and we fulfilled the contract."

Suddenly, Saul realized the connection between the wireless bridges and the drugs in Galina's apartment. "You said your *organic* researchers came through. I take it, then, that part of the contract called for synthesis of an instant recovery drug."

Michelle peered at him over the top of her champagne glass, the way a bombardier would fix sights on an enemy below. "Sweetheart, you missed your calling in life. You should have gone on the pro jigsaw-puzzle circuit."

"Galina Rosmanov gained access to the drug. She could have gained access to the bridges, too."

"Perhaps so, but I hardly think she had one with her when she left Mexico City. Saul, those things are immense. Unless you've seen one, you have no conception. They're as big as skyscrapers."

"Granted, she didn't have an actual wireless bridge. But suppose she had the *plans* for one."

Michelle refilled her glass and savored the liquid's bouquet. Refinement in the face of adversity, the hallmark of nobility. "Impossible. The plans themselves would fill a good-sized library."

"All right. Let's say she had microfilm records of the plans. How's that?"

"We never made any, so she couldn't have stolen them from us. And even if she could have accessed our storage facilities, no easy feat in itself, it would have taken her months to shoot those plans onto microfilm. You wouldn't believe the number of documents involved."

Saul sat down on the sofa and rubbed his eyes with his hands. For a few hours after transfer, recovery tablets boosted energy levels. Then a mild, short-lived depression set in. Too many of the tablets over too short a time span multiplied this depression, stretching it out to hours, sometimes days. For that reason, the Bridge Authority recommended no more than one transfer per day. Saul had made nine in the past seventy-two hours and was having increasing difficulty shaking off the aftereffects. "O.K. Let's assume she did not have a portable wireless bridge. But she had something almost as good. She got somebody *believing* she had a portable wireless bridge. She shows them a phony movie, whips the instant recovery drug past them, and winds up with a buyer. Word then filters down that she's about to sell an operational portable wireless bridge to a hardcore radical group. Say One World United. Given that set of circumstances, who would be anxious to stop her?"

Michelle swept her hand grandiosely around, as though the room were packed with people. "Anyone in their right mind."

"Explain that."

"Gladly." She poured out the last of the champagne, went to the door, signaled her waiter, and ordered another bottle. "Suppose it were possible for One World United to construct and operate a net of truly portable wireless bridges. Suppose they blanketed the world with them. What would happen? Well, first of all, national boundaries disappear. Great for OWU. That's what they've been yearning for all along. But what kind of chaos does it inflict on the rest of the world?"

She walked to a window. Near-destitute vendors lined the street outside, competing fiercely for the few spare pesos of the equally poor people passing by. "If those people down there had a magic carpet able to transport them anywhere on earth, where do you think they would be? Here in the back alleys of Mexico City? Or in Palm Springs? Miami Beach? Cape Cod? The Côte d'Azur? Imagine it, Saul. Hordes of poor ravaging the world like clouds of locust. Searching for a nirvana that doesn't exist. Like it or not, people in underdeveloped countries have grown accustomed to a modest standard of living. Is it fair to give them open access to something they are not prepared to handle? We transfer a million dying beggars from the streets of Calcutta to the streets of San Francisco. Is that progress?"

The waiter arrived with the new bottle of champagne, opened it, and left. Michelle pulled it out of its silver bucket, picked up a glass in the same hand, opened the door to the bathroom slightly, and passed both inside exhibiting the same expression of benign guilt seen on elderly matrons passing table scraps to a poodle. "Next point. The world makes a pretty big hiding place. With an open, unsecured system of portable wireless bridges, crooks, assassins, kidnappers, smugglers, would have a field day. They could strike at will and then hop off instantly.

"And what about taxation. Taxes support a tremendous portion of our social welfare programs. What happens to them when national boundaries vanish?

"Plus there will come vultures. People who will buy up currently inaccessible land, develop it, install a wireless bridge, and watch the land skyrocket in value. What will that do to ecology? To have housing developments sprouting in every forest? On top of every mountain? Overlooking every waterfall?

"No question about it, Saul. Development of a truly portable wireless bridge would turn society topsy-turvy overnight. I'll be totally frank. If you asked me how far I would go to prevent that from happening, my answer would move me straight to the head of your suspect list. Granted, sales and maintenance of a portable wireless bridge would prove quite lucrative to us. But how much would it really improve service? According to my technical advisers, it is impossible to transmit travelers through the air any faster than we transmit them through wire. Hence, a portable wireless bridge wouldn't increase transmission speed in the slightest. It would, however, decentralize transportal control thus giving rise to safety problems of the first magnitude. Why pioneer a potentially dangerous new technique when the existing one is already more than adequate?" She extended one leg in front of the other, like a tennis player preparing to vault the net just after having scored match point. "But the whole argument is academic anyway, since I know for a fact that there is no such thing as a portable wireless bridge and probably will not be for decades to come.

"Now, if you have nothing else, I'd like to resume my dinner."

Saul nodded. Too many things still didn't add up. Michelle's sudden and decidedly untypical concern with service and efficiency to the exclusion of corporate profits. Her earlier cryptic inference that Galina posed a danger to civilization. Mary Hemke's certainty that what she saw in Galina's movie was truly a portable wireless bridge.

Despite even Herman's belief to the contrary, was it just possible that the portable wireless bridge really did exist?

One thing for sure. He would have to go elsewhere for the answer. He would never find out from Michelle.

He draped his tie over the railing outside Michelle's door and left it to dangle there, still and lifeless, like the becalmed standard of a stifled army.

CHAPTER 14

"If there was a portable wireless bridge," Saul said to Herman, "it would consist of two transportals. Maybe Galina broke up the set. Sold one to OWU and one to somebody else. Maybe that somebody else wanted an exclusive and, to get it, decided to head off the second sale at the pass."

"That's good theory," said Herman. "But there's another possibility that plays equally well. Suppose Galina did have two wireless transportals. Both phony. She sold the first one to a buyer who quickly spotted it for a fake. So that buyer shows her what happens to con artists who peddle shoddy merchandise to the big boys."

Logical. Saul should have thought of it himself. But his mental efficiency had fallen far below normal. He was neglecting pertinent data, missing obvious alternatives. Too many transfers in too short a time. And still no end in sight.

Rosie was seated in a corner, her head down, her eyes shut. The casual observer would have assumed she had dozed off, but Saul knew better. Contrary to the traditional detective's *modus operandi,* she found her best clues with her eyes closed. "Check out the other big-name matter transference scientists," she said. "Maybe the first buyer brought the bridge to one of them for evaluation. Or maybe one of them actually built it."

Another obvious possibility overlooked. Perhaps Saul had best take a break. Relax for a while. Permit his bruised mind to recuperate. But then he looked at the clock Herman had rigged up over the computer. It flashed a downward progression of numbers signifying Herman's estimate of the amount of time remaining in Galina Rosmanov's life. The indicator stood at just a bit over forty-six hours. "Herman," Saul said, "name me everybody you know who would be scientifically capable of evaluating or building a portable wireless bridge."

Herman wiggled around in his chair, trying in vain to find a position that would relieve his growing physical discomfort. He could have used a good shoulder massage, but there was no one to administer it. His girlfriend, her patience finally exhausted, had left the collector station about an hour ago. She had been more than willing to play house with Herman, but not if their roles were mother and invalid child. "You're chasing shadows, Saul. The matter-transference field is a small community. Rumors spread like wildfire. If anyone had seen or been working on a portable wireless bridge I certainly would have heard something about it. But I haven't."

Saul rubbed his thumb and first two fingers together. "If you want to guarantee a closed mouth, there's no better glue than money."

Herman responded reluctantly, like someone forced to walk a dog in the rain. "There are two men, a Japanese and an Israeli. Both under contract to the Bridge Authority. We've worked together from time to time, and they both impressed me as smart boys. Their names are Omura Takahashi and Sammy Blonder."

"Any idea where they live?"

"Omura in the Andes someplace. Sammy, I think, in Rio."

Samuel Blonder resided in an extremely exclusive section of Rio, just off the Alemeda. His large villa had all the charm of a live-in vault. It incorporated every security device on the market. A high stone wall topped with an electronic anti-intrusion fence. Uniformed guards both inside and outside the fence perimeter. A double-doored front gate with triangulated TV surveillance. Roving guard dogs. Either Blonder owned, or Blonder was, something very valuable.

A guard at the gate took Saul's credentials, passed them under a glowing light that presumably spotted alterations, then double-checked by calling Bridge Authority headquarters. When Saul proved out, the guard signaled two other guards who escorted him from the gate to the front door. The guards had the hard-boiled bearing of mercenaries, men who responded with rifles and up-turned palms to the blowing of other people's bugles.

Blonder greeted Saul at the front door. His compact, muscular body vibrated with nervous energy. His feet bubbled up and down on the marble floor. His remarkably slender fingers hopped from pocket to pocket like five-beaked hummingbirds flitting through a patch of clover. He kept glancing nervously around, at the ceiling, the floor, the walls, as though his every movement was being observed, his every word monitored. Saul had seen men act like this before, but they had all worn manacles around their legs, attached by chains to the walls of a detention cell in a maximum-security prison.

Blonder ushered Saul into the living room.

During his marriage to Michelle, Saul had been dragged against his will to dinners and parties at a number of opulent mansions. But never had he been in a residence as lavish as this. Exceptionally fine paintings and statues everywhere, most of them done by artists so famous even Saul recognized their work. Subtle lighting. Expensive antiques. Saul wondered which came over more often, the upholsterer who tightened the creases and shampooed the blemishes out of the furniture, or the plastic surgeon who performed much the same function for Blonder's face.

"Can I get you a drink?" Blonder asked.

Even though he knew he would suffer for it his next transfer, Saul asked for a double scotch neat.

Blonder poured two, and passed one to Saul. "What can I do for you Mr. Lukas? On the phone you mentioned something about portable wireless bridges."

"Yes. I'd like to get your opinions concerning the probability of developing such devices."

"Oh, we'll have them," Blonder said confidently. "Someday. We'll get the big breakthrough and somebody will do it."

"You don't think it's been done already?"

"Most assuredly not." Blonder spaced his words out evenly like the final dribbles of time given off by a discarded clock. "You see, at one point several years ago I became fascinated with the prospect of building a portable wireless bridge. To the matter-transference scientist I suppose it's the equivalent of chasing down the

Holy Grail. There probably isn't one of us who hasn't actively pursued the idea at some point or other in his career. I worked on it for quite a while with what I would call a modest degree of success. I came up with several mathematical relationships which, I felt, if properly applied, would overcome several of the technical limitations involved. I never took them to the practical stage, however." Blonder slowed his speech even more, like a man reading aloud that section of a history book dealing with his own reputation.

"The Bridge Authority is not anxious to pursue a portable wireless bridge. You see, as long as they control the wires, they control world transportation. Take away the wires, and you remove the major source of their power. The Bridge Authority will go to great lengths to prevent that from happening." Blonder interlaced his fingers into a cup that he held in front of his body, ready to snap stray concepts out of the air and crush them before they could sprout wings and soar away. "There is a great deal of money to be made by *not* pursuing findings relating to portable wireless bridges." He picked up a nearby *objet d'art,* hefted it disinterestedly and set it back on its pedestal like a child, bored, even though trapped in a playpen filled with toys.

"If someone gave you a device which they said was a portable wireless bridge, would you be capable of judging its authenticity?"

"I would certainly hope so." Blonder placed an elbow on his mantelpiece and posed there beneath numerous photographs taken of himself together with some of the most scholarly men in the world. Intelligence by association, the principle underlying higher education since the world began.

"And has anyone given you such a task recently? Has anyone brought you a portable wireless bridge for evaluation? A device which you, perhaps, found to be fraudulent?"

"No, I'm afraid not."

"You're certain. Within the past few weeks you've examined no portable wireless bridges, real or otherwise?"

"Absolutely not."

Saul opened his briefcase and pulled out the notebook he had found in Galina's apartment. "Ever seen this before?"

Blonder looked at the scientific notations inside and smiled

rather wistfully, as though remembering the pleasures of a long-
gone summer. "I wrote these equations myself. This is my notebook."

Definitely not the answer Saul had expected. "You're a hydroelectronic engineer?" he asked stunned.

"I don't understand. Hydroelectronic engineer? What has that
got to do with these? These are the notes I told you about. The
ones dealing with the construction of a portable wireless bridge.
The last I heard, the Bridge Authority had them in a storage vault
someplace."

"You're sure. You're absolutely sure these are your notes?"

"Mr. Lukas, I can certainly recognize my own work when I
see it."

The question was, Why couldn't Herman?

CHAPTER 15

Omura Takahashi added nothing new to Saul's knowledge. Like Blonder, he too lived in a grand, smartly furnished villa. Heavily guarded. He too had done preliminary research into portable wireless bridges. He too had been persuaded to channel his energies elsewhere.

But he had not built a portable wireless bridge, neither had anyone approached him with a request to evaluate one.

When shown Blonder's equations, Takahashi held them gingerly by the edges, as though they were holy gospel inscribed on a swatch of fragile papyrus recently unearthed from the bowels of a Middle Eastern cave.

Needless to say, he grasped their significance immediately.

Herman, hunched over the collector station's computer terminal keyboard, grew increasingly frustrated with his inability to accomplish the simplest of calculations with any degree of precision. His fingers responded like pudgy earthworms, squirming haphazardly through a compost heap of plastic numbers. He continually had to punch the terminal's reset key to cancel out his progressively worsening errors.

Saul came up behind him and poked at his shoulder, but Herman, totally absorbed in the vain attempt to get his computations to jibe with the red-lined computer printout taped to the wall beside him, did not repond.

Normally, Saul would have left Herman to his work and returned later when Herman was free. But not today. Today he grabbed Herman by the shoulder and jerked him roughly around on his stool. So much for professional courtesy.

"Hey! What do you think you're doing?" Herman wailed. "You

just blew my data chain. I'll have to start it completely from scratch."

Herman's eyes bulged out of their sockets with the cockeyed muddiness of two flower bulbs washed to the surface by a heavy spring rain. He was so obviously ill that Saul was tempted to postpone their confrontation long enough to call in a doctor. Then the clock overhead flashed the fact that Galina Rosmanov had only thirty-one hours of life remaining. "I think it's time we had a heart to heart," Saul said, snagging Herman under the armpit and hauling him to his feet. "In private."

Saul half-carried, half-dragged Herman to the programming supervisor's office, a glassed-in cubicle overlooking the computer room. He deposited Herman into the closest chair and kicked shut the door. He put his index finger against Herman's chest and poked it hard to emphasize each succeeding word. "I want Galina Rosmanov brought out, and I want her brought out now."

A ruddy flush etched deep crevices of chagrin into Herman's face. "The equations. You hadn't been gone half an hour when I remembered you had the equations." Herman slapped the back of one hand into the palm of the other like an embarrassed chess master bemoaning an amateurishly lost game. "You showed the equations to Blonder and he identified them."

"Right on the button." Saul grabbed Herman by the shirt front and pulled him partially out of his chair. "You and I have been friends for quite a while. But if you think that's going to save you, old buddy, you're wrong. If that girl in there dies, I'll see you hang for murder."

Herman's mouth popped open and closed, then screwed into a sour pucker, as though he had for the first time tasted the disgrace of criminal liability. "You think I can get her out anytime I want to. You think I'm keeping her in there on purpose. To cover up my own involvement."

Saul pushed him back down. "That's how I read it. I don't know if you got her in there, but I'm convinced you know how to get her out."

Herman swung his head vigorously from shoulder to shoulder. "Not true. Not true."

Saul wanted desperately to believe that, but found it impossible to do so. There was simply too much evidence to the contrary.

"Let's start at the beginning. You built that working pair of portable bridges. Correct?"

Herman sat up straight in his chair, a seedling of pride sprouting from out of a forest of pretenses. "Yes. I recognized their feasibility several years ago. I approached the Bridge Authority and suggested they set me up as head of a developmental project team. Instead they offered me twenty million dollars and a castle in France to forget about it. They made it quite clear that should I decline their offer they would deny me access to the bridge network. That, in essence, would have meant the end of my career. So I agreed.

"Since then they've kept me under constant surveillance. Guards surround my house. My research is monitored. A Bridge Authority official is present whenever I discuss matter transference with a colleague. They tap my phone calls. They attend my lectures, read my articles prior to publication. They want to make absolutely certain I don't succumb to the urge to resume work on a portable wireless bridge."

Saul tilted his head quizzically. "If you were being watched that closely, how did you manage to develop the portable wireless bridge anyway?"

Herman flashed a real dazzler of a smile, the kind he reserved exclusively for use on TV talk shows and at international award banquets. Competence well laced with youthful exuberance. The eternal boy scout.

"It was quite simple, actually. You see the Bridge Authority conceived of wireless bridges in terms of the wireless network they already had. Exceedingly complex, requiring voluminous amounts of power, based on technologies incorporating certain hard-to-get materials. Dreyfus crystals, for instance, and high-frequency galenium arsenide transmitters. That's what they watched for. But I fooled them. My bridges don't use those materials. My bridges don't even use the same design technologies as the military's wireless network. I developed a totally new system, as different from the military net as that one is from the commercial net we have now. I came up with a pair of small, simple, and extremely economical portable wireless bridges. In quantity, the cost of manufacturing one shouldn't exceed a hundred dollars."

As far as Saul was concerned, everything Herman had said thus far was no more than background for the real question. "How did Galina Rosmanov fit into this?"

Herman crossed his arms on his knees and rested his chin on them, his rolled-up shirtsleeves forming a cushion for either side of his head. "I had just begun my work when I met her. At a party given by a mutual acquaintance. Heinrich Boehm, the German surgeon. It was like something from out of a movie. Eyes meeting across a crowded room. An unspoken invitation. Soft whispers. A walk on the terrace. A night of lovemaking in a picturesque French country inn. From then on we saw each other every chance we got. Always in secret, of course. A different city every time. Out-of-the-way hotels. Too great a chance of censure if it ever became public knowledge that an American scientist was having an affair with a Russian ballerina. Inevitably, as we grew closer, I told Galina about my work on the portable wireless bridge. I said I had the theory completely worked out in my head, and I could build an operational model at will. She asked me what was stopping me, and I told her that the construction would require some fairly exotic and expensive machinery. Stuff I couldn't afford. The next time I saw her, I believe it was three or four days later, she told me that she had found someone willing to finance me. The One World United group. I don't know if you've heard of them. I hadn't."

Not surprising. Herman rarely if ever read newspapers. He was less interested in the world as it was than in the world as it could be. "You must have been one of the few."

Herman wagged his hand in front of his forehead to convey clarity of conscience. "I didn't know who they were, and frankly I didn't care. Galina said they would provide me with the money I needed. In return they wanted two working prototypes. They promised to mass-produce them and distribute them to the world. Exactly the opposite of how the Bridge Authority would have treated them. So I agreed."

The unbalanced teeter-totter world of politics and science. The politicians using their considerable bulk to keep the scientists dangling in the air. Then along comes OWU with a ladder, a scientist scrambles down, and suddenly the playground becomes a graveyard. "Do you know where One World United got the money to finance this project of yours?"

"No."

Saul leaned forward, put one hand on either arm of Herman's chair, and spit his words directly into Herman's face. "They held children for ransom. They robbed banks. They contracted for murders. They pushed drugs. Sort of the James gang with a social cause."

Herman pushed out his forearm, as though it bore a magical ribbon bestowed by a sorcerer to keep knights and crusaders incorruptible on their pilgrimages to save the world. "That's not my concern. I personally did nothing wrong. I have nothing to be ashamed of."

"I seem to recall other people who felt the same way. They wore swastikas and averted their eyes while their comrades turned people into lampshades."

Herman extended his hands and molded thin air into a vision of a better future. "Saul, if you ever saw those bridges, you'd understand. They advance scientific knowledge by decades. What do I care who paid for them? It's the end product, the result that matters. Those bridges are absolutely marvelous. Perfectly safe. They totally eliminate the problem of misalignment. In fact they're so safe I would ride them myself. They require only an infinitesimal amount of power, a single ten-volt, self-contained battery pack does it. They're such an improvement over what we have now that I can barely dredge up enough superlatives. The world must have them. They must be made available freely to everyone everywhere."

His sermon produced no convert here. Saul cared about portable wireless bridges only insofar as they directly involved one person, Galina Rosmanov. "How did Galina get hold of Blonder's notes?"

"I don't know." Herman pinched the bridge of his nose between his thumb and index finger. "I noticed them missing from out of my briefcase one day. I'm constantly losing papers anyway, so I didn't consider it unusual. No one but an expert could have deciphered them. Besides, I had gone beyond them by then anyway, so I had no real need to get them back.

"As a consultant to the Bridge Authority I had open access to all files and documents in the Bridge Authority's confiscation file. That's where they keep the documents they buy up from scientists who threaten major breakthroughs. Most of those scientists were way off on unimportant tangents. But a few, like Blonder, had really stumbled onto something. Given adequate time and sufficient money, one of them might have been able to carry it off. Build a portable wireless bridge. Of course, the Bridge Authority would never let anyone get that far."

"What about the drugs? The ones I found in Galina's apartment?"

Inexplicably, in light of everything else Herman had done, this was the first thing that seemed to provoke any evidence of shame. "Those I stole. To make the portable wireless bridge a practical short-distance commute method, I needed something to compress recovery time. The drugs were it. I knew about them from my work on the military wireless network. So one evening I broke into the organic lab and stole some. Since I suspect the Bridge Authority comes snooping through my place when I'm not around, I gave them to Galina for safekeeping."

"What about the other stuff? The powder we haven't identified yet?"

"I have no idea what that is or where it came from. It has nothing to do with me."

Saul paused in his interrogation long enough to light a cigarette. "This portable wireless bridge of yours," he said, his words punching through the cloud of smoke enveloping his face, "how does it work?"

Herman plumped out his chest, a proud father bragging about the exploits of a precocious child. "Each bridge gets assigned a number. Like a telephone number. To travel, you punch in your number and the number of the transportal you want to reach. Your transportal locks to the other and gives you a red-light confirmation that a bridge has been established. You step inside, punch the send button, and you're transmitted. That's all there is to it. Simplicity personified. It doesn't need collector stations since the earth's magnetic field doesn't perturb the signal the way it does in the wire network, though I don't fully understand why.

"I still have some minor work left, but nothing complicated. For instance, while the system doesn't require much power to send or receive, it does take a good healthy jolt to warm it up, so it's more efficient to start it once and then leave it permanently on. I still have to figure a way to lock out incoming matter. Otherwise, if you had one set up in your house, crooks or anybody could come in at will. But that's just a minor problem, easy enough to overcome once I get a spare minute to devote to it. Right now I've already started work on the next generation. A bridge that doesn't require a transportal. It will operate via a pocket-sized control unit. Ship you anyplace you want to go. And I've almost got it, Saul. I've almost got it."

Again Saul ignored the allure of scientific achievement in favor of the rather mundane pursuit of relevant fact. "How many transportals did you build?"

"Two."

"And where are they now?"

"Galina had them, for the same reason she had the drugs. So the Bridge Authority wouldn't stumble on them in a search of my apartment."

Saul began to pace, six steps in one direction, six in the other, so precise in his movements, a piano student could have used him for a metronome. "These transportals. How big are they?"

Herman held his hands almost exactly as far apart as Mary Hemke had held hers. "About two feet by eighteen inches. They were only prototypes. Production models would be bigger."

Six steps one way, six the other. "So one of these devices would fit into a steamer trunk?"

"Sure. Easily. In fact both of them would."

"Therefore it's conceivable that Galina may have had one or both with her when she entered the wires?"

"Entirely possible, although I don't know why she'd be carting them around. We both agreed to keep them hidden until I had them fully perfected and ready to turn over."

Saul finished his cigarette and lit another from the butt. "You said these portable bridges are self-powered and are never shut off."

"Correct."

Saul stopped his pacing. His cigarette, clenched between his fingers, arched through the air, a glowing quill orchestrating a symphony of intrigue and evil. "Let's call those bridges A and B.

Now suppose that Galina had bridge A with her, packed in her trunk. Further suppose that either accidently or on purpose someone fed something from bridge B into bridge A, just as the trunk that held it was being fed into a conventional bridge."

Herman rubbed at his eyelids, tugging them down in a hopeless attempt to relieve some of the burning caused by the horrible redness beneath. "An interesting hypothesis."

Saul shook his head. "It may not be as hypothetical as you think. What precisely would be the end result of a situation like that?"

Herman scribed an imaginary line across the arm of his chair, a line representing an orderly progression of events. "Well, if something like that happened, it would radically alter the gross weight of the portable bridge. It would disrupt the transmission. The portable unit would in essence swell up inside the wire like a sponge in a water pipe."

"And anything else in there with it would be blocked in, too."

Herman dropped his chin to his chest. "Yes."

"Is that what happened to Galina Rosmanov?"

Once more Herman dropped his chin. "So I suspect."

Saul exploded. Anger, which ate at his gut, was much easier for him to suppress than betrayal, which attacked his heart. "And exactly how *long* have you suspected it?"

Herman's reddening face gave Saul the answer even before Herman spoke the words. "Since about an hour after I got here. The signs were quite obvious if you knew what to look for."

"Yet you didn't tell me."

Herman tried to grab Saul's arm to establish a direct link between them, but Saul pulled away. "I was afraid to," Herman said. "If the Bridge Authority finds out that I know how to construct a portable wireless bridge, I truly believe they'll kill me to repress the knowledge."

"So, to protect yourself, you're letting Galina Rosmanov die in the wires." Saul cut through the inner complexities and got right to the final extreme.

"It's not like that, Saul." Again Herman grabbed for Saul's arm, except this time he reached it before Saul could pull away. Once he had it, he clung to it like a falling mountaineer grasping for life onto the only outcropping on an otherwise sheer cliff. "I have really done everything possible to get her out. I really have. Really."

Saul gave no indication that he either believed or disbelieved that statement. "You say you built two of these portable wireless bridges, both to be delivered to the OWU."

"Right."

"Yet when I spoke to the OWU, they said Galina had promised them only one. A single unit. That means she had probably intended to peddle the second unit elsewhere. And whoever she sold it to used it against her."

Herman shook his head. "No, never. Galina wouldn't do that to me. I mean she *loved* me." For all his erudition, a remarkably backward man when it came to the basic workings of human nature.

"Let's just suppose for a second that she could. Any idea who that second party might have been?"

Herman thought for a moment before responding. "I haven't the slightest idea."

"She never gave you so much as a hint?"

"No. Nothing." Herman glanced at the clock over the terminal and struggled to his feet. "Would you excuse me? I have a timed experiment going, and it's about ready for checking."

Vigorously, Saul shook his head. "I'm afraid somebody else will have to follow through. You're finished on this project."

Herman looked anxiously at the clock, then back at Saul. "I've told you the truth. Like it or not, Saul, I'm the only one who can save that girl."

"I'm going to give Sammy Blonder a chance to disprove that."

"Saul, Blonder's strictly second-rate. He'll blow it."

Saul stood. "Perhaps so, but at least I'll know he gave it his best shot." Saul picked up the office phone and, taking one of the hardest actions of his life, instructed station security to take Herman Lindstrom into custody.

CHAPTER 16

The two-hundred-foot-high spherical collector rested atop a black steel pedestal outfitted with triply redundant Monroe hydraulic levelers. Automatic sensors and frequency diverters ringed the pedestal's outer edge. In the event of a massive tilt, in transference tolerances anything greater than one one-hundredth of a degree, these diverters would cut in to shut down the collector and route traffic through alternate lines.

Moving stairs whisked Saul past this safeguard apparatus to the top of the pedestal where he walked the fifteen yards to the one point where a reasonably tall man such as himself could reach up and touch the globe proper. A globe, probably more than any other single constructed entity, epitomized the sophistication of the Bridge Authority's manufacturing techniques. Each globe required nearly two full years to complete. According to the Bridge Authority's public relations department, which seemingly had a full-time staff dedicated to formulating unlikely comparisons, each globe contained enough raw materials to construct either a twenty-five-story office building, a U. S. Navy destroyer, or a Pluto rocket. Again according to the Bridge Authority, if the integrated circuits incorporated into the globe were removed and set end to end (presumably with the aid of extremely tiny tweezers), they would form a subminiature strand long enough to twice encircle the world. Scientists spent months running transference simulations through this circuitry before declaring it fit to go on-line. Even then, the globe did not process passengers until it had run on twice normal power for sixty consecutive days without so much as a brown-down.

To insure precise refocusing of the beam, buffing specialists spent thousands of hours hand-polishing the great globe's inner surface. The outer surface, because it had no effect upon the transmission process, got only enough machining to put a dull sheen on its natural green-gold finish.

Saul was surprised when he touched that finish to find it ice cold. During normal operation the globe's outer surface was typically at least twenty degrees warmer than the ambient air. Each traveler passing through raised the collector's internal temperature an average of one-half degree. A subsurface matrix of heat exchangers vented off this warmth. Since the collector was now off-line, there was none of this internal heat to dissipate. It was eerie touching a cold collector, rather like feeling for fever on the forehead of a dead man.

Saul rapped the collector with his knuckles like a spiritualist attempting to contact a ghost residing within the walls of a haunted house. So much lay locked inside this great sphere. Galina Rosmanov, certainly, but also, with her, the complex bits of information necessary to set her free. For instance, Herman believed One World United had financed construction of his portable wireless bridge. But Mary Hemke told Saul she had committed to buy the finished product. Nothing more. So if One World United hadn't funded Herman, who had? The Russians? The Israelis? Or somebody else? There was certainly no shortage of governments and organizations with the right qualifiers, big bucks and an awesome yen for power.

Saul rubbed the collector again, but no magic genie sprang forth to solve his riddle. Even Rosie had drawn a blank on this one. She had spent twelve full hours up here in a maximum effort to establish positive contact with the trapped ballerina, but to no avail. She had gotten nothing except a repetition of the impression she had picked up before. Galina Rosmanov was happy inside. Not only couldn't she come out, she didn't want to.

A young girl entered through the double revolving doors that maintained the building's precisely monitored temperature. She held an armload of file folders across her breast as though they might offer her some margin of protection in the event of a physical attack. "Mr. Lukas," she said hesitantly as she approached Saul. "Here are the records you asked for." She extended the files with the reluctance of a veterinarian performing throat surgery on an unsedated lion. Everyone in the Bridge Authority knew of the Resurrectionist and his volatile abuse of subordinates who performed less than perfectly. Company employees went to great lengths to avoid dealing with him.

The girl, a high school student working for the Bridge Authority part-time, had, by virtue of her complete lack of seniority, drawn the unpleasant duty this round.

She need not have worried. Saul barely acknowledged her presence. The entire time she was with him his eyes never once left the globe.

On her way out, she glanced at the globe herself to see what it was about it that so engrossed him. But it looked no different from the dozens of others she had seen. A great metallic marble, although this one didn't ping the way the others did. Yet the way he looked at it you'd think it was a crystal ball about to tell him the state of the world tomorrow.

Saul banged his hand against the globe one last time, carried the file to a nearby table, opened it, and spread out its contents. The file contained a computerized log of every bridge ticket made out to Galina Rosmanov in the past six months.

Saul pulled another list out of his pocket. This one itemized the Kirov Ballet's schedule for that same time frame. He laid the two lists side by side. With his pen he crossed off tickets corresponding to performances. Then he eliminated tickets to her home cities, Rome and Madrid. Next he ran down the list and dropped out every city Galina had visited only once during the period. These he assumed to be either shopping trips, meetings with Mary Hemke, or liaisons with Herman. That left him with thirty-eight trips. Five each to Tokyo and Peking, four each to Tel Aviv and Beirut, twenty to Washington, D.C. The trips to Tokyo, Peking, Tel Aviv, and Beirut had come early during the period. The trips to Washington had begun after the others ceased, and had continued right up until the end. The pattern suggested that she had sounded out several potential buyers before entering into serious negotiations. The fact that the negotiating locale seemed to have been Washington suggested the final buyer had been the United States. But that could have been a ploy to divert suspicion from a totally different country.

Saul walked to the collector station's transportal. Since it normally handled only the comings and goings of station personnel, it hadn't gotten the glamour treatment the Bridge Authority lavished on regular passenger units. The transportal's sides and top were natural metallic rather than wood-veneered. The slip padding inside was upholstered with heavy-duty denim rather than the more expensive and less durable plastic velour. The transportal itself was crammed innocuously into a tiny room located between two collector sphere power banks. There was normally neither a hostess nor a full-time operator on duty at the transportal, although since the station had become the center for the effort to free Galina Rosmanov, round-the-clock shifts of each had been imported.

Saul sat impatiently through the hostess' speech, swallowed his pill, passed through weigh-in, and entered the transportal. The world dissolved into a blue haze around him, and he awoke an hour later in Washington.

He emerged from the recovery room ravenously hungry. In thinking about it, he realized he couldn't remember the last time he had eaten. He checked one of the local wall clocks to see what meal would be appropriate. The clock read 5:30 A.M. Breakfast.

While he had a plastic-encased pass that would gain him access to the exclusive gourmet dining room maintained in the terminal for use by top-level Bridge Authority management, he chose, as he always did, to eat with the paying travelers in the terminal's regular downstairs snack bar.

The snack bar was located in the first subbasement, immediately above the terminal's computer room. The doorway duplicated the entry into a transportal.

Saul went through and took a seat at the counter. The place was decorated in what Saul called public relations modern. Framed newspaper headlines proclaimed milestones in bridge development. "Matter transmitted through wire," said one. "First transcontinental passenger wire installed," said another. "Worldwide bridge network officially completed," read a third. Tabletops had been constructed out of Plexiglas-covered cross sections of bundled wire.

Saul picked up a menu. Since diners could be from any time

zone around the world, the snack bar served breakfast, lunch, and dinner concurrently throughout the day. The public relations department had apparently penned the menu, too, since it listed such items as the Transportal Tuna Sandwich and the Speed-of-Lightning Omelette.

Saul ordered two carob breakfast bars (the Super-Zap Special) and coffee. He opened the newspaper he had picked up on the way in. He skipped most of the hard news, spent the better part of one carob bar on sports and the comics, then finished up with the feature section.

The lead story concerned an Eskimo whom the newspaper had transported to Miami Beach. Saul read through the first paragraph, up to the point where great fun was made of the man's becoming sick to his stomach on baked Alaska. Saul left the remainder of his carob bar on his plate, stuffed the paper into the trash bin on the far side of the counter, paid his bill, and left.

From the snack bar he went to personnel. Records there informed him that the last time Galina Rosmanov had visited Washington she had been handled by a hostess named Nacy Lee, an expatriot Finn who, according to her file, had barely managed to get out of the country before the Russian invasion. A check with crew scheduling told Saul the girl was currently on duty inside the terminal.

When he found her, she was reassuring her charge, a pregnant woman, that the trip would do no damage to her unborn baby, that wire technology was fully able to keep track of more than one physiology at a time. Saul waited until the pregnant woman had boarded her wire, then identified himself to Nacy Lee and told her of his interest in Galina Rosmanov.

He asked Nacy to recall for him, if she could, anything unusual that might have occurred during Galina's last visit to Washington. After some contemplation, Nacy told Saul that Galina had been in normal spirits, not exceptionally happy nor exceptionally sad. Outside of a few general observations concerning the weather, Galina hadn't spoken at all.

It looked as though Saul's trip to Washington, admittedly a long shot, had wound up a total waste of time. He thanked Nacy and started down the hall.

"Oh, Mr. Lukas," said Nacy, calling him back. "There was one thing. I almost forgot. She did ask me to call her a cab. I overheard her giving the cabbie her destination, and I thought it rather odd."

Saul returned to her side. "How so?"

"Well, I mean her being a *Russian* and all." Nacy rubbed at the lapel of her hostess jacket, as if trying to eradicate a blemish. "I mean what business could a *Russian* possibly have at Bridge Authority Headquarters?"

CHAPTER 17

"He's coming around, Doctor." The voice rubbed across his inert mind like a swatch of silk, aligning into neat rows whatever it was that gave him vitality and animation.

"Thank God." If the first voice had been silk, this one was burlap, rough, untextured, shredded from age. "Can you imagine the board review I'd face if I lost the Resurrectionist?"

Saul opened his eyes. He could feel metallic pincers clamped across his arms, legs, and midsection like calipers measuring him up for a burial suit. A thick white haze enveloped his head. He tried to bring a hand up to wave it away, but neither hand would move; both were securely strapped to the side of his bed.

Life monitors, for which the pincers acted as pickups, reacted to his attempted motion by instantly activating a pump that evacuated the haze, a resuscitative medication administered through the respiratory system. The clear plastic tent covering him from head to waist opened and a nurse poked her upper torso in and positioned his arm so the burlap-voiced doctor could extract the feed-in to the blood analyzer. "Well, Mr. Lukas," said the doctor as he worked, "you gave us quite a scare. We were afraid you were going to book one-way passage on that big wire to the sky." The doctor laughed uproariously at his rather macabre joke. He wasn't bothered in the least that no one else joined in. He was a man quite used to laughing alone. He disconnected the pincers, unstrapped Saul's arms, and helped him to a sitting position. "Tell me, Mr. Lucas, how many trips through the wires would you estimate you've taken in the past few days?"

Saul tried to count them, but couldn't differentiate one from the next with enough clarity to get a firm fix. It even took him a moment to sort out the last one, Washington to Mexico City, the one that had landed him here in this bed. "I don't know. Twelve. Maybe more."

The doctor swung his head back and forth, his eyes wide with a mixture of abhorrence and fascination, like a man watching a tennis match between the Angel of Death and the Grim Reaper. "That's quite far above the recommended limit. For your own good, I suggest you remain here for observation. Until we can be sure you haven't suffered any permanent internal damage."

Saul rubbed his wrists together, and swung his feet over the side of the bed. "Sorry, Doc. Impossible." He stood up. Had the nurse not been at his side to steady him, he would have promptly collapsed.

"Mr. Lukas," said the doctor. "You really ought not to leave."

"Afraid I don't have any choice." Saul pulled on his shirt and, with inordinately great difficulty, buttoned it.

The doctor spread his hands apart, palms upward, and gazed toward the ceiling, as though on the lookout for the first drops of misfortune bound to rain down on anyone ignoring his counsel. "I can't keep you here against your will. However, I can give you a word of advice. If you want to stay alive, stay out of the wires for at least two, better yet three weeks." The doctor coiled up his stethoscope and tucked it into his pocket alongside the shriveled remnants of any further obligation.

From a phone in the dispensary's outer office, Saul called Sammy Blonder at the collector station. "How's it going?" Saul asked.

The volume of commotion in the background sounded more appropriate to an automotive assembly plant than to a collector station computer room. "Not so hot, Saul. Like you asked, I brought in a triple shift and set them to work independently rechecking Lindstrom's figures."

"And?" Saul's last hope. Perhaps in covering up his own involvement, Herman had lied about the true seriousness of Galina Rosmanov's predicament. Maybe she wasn't really as securely stuck in the wires as Herman had made her out to be.

"Sorry, Saul." Blonder spoke gently. He knew this wasn't what

Saul wanted to hear. "Everything Lindstrom told you was true. Nearly as I can figure, he didn't lay back a bit. He did his honest best to get her out."

Saul smacked a hand against a nearby wall. There were two things he regretted seeing disappear as the world progressed to ever-increasing levels of impersonal technological complexity. The free lunch and the easy solution. "Thanks, Sammy. Let me know if anything changes."

Saul grabbed a cab from the terminal into Mexico City to the Paseo de Robles, Michelle's hotel. Despite mediocre food and service, smallish rooms, and highly exorbitant prices, it was far and away the favorite of international dignitaries and important business people. The reason? A unique extra service. The Paseo de Robles had a security system more penetration-resistant than 75 per cent of the world's top military command posts. Each floor boasted a complete electronic surveillance web, everything from in-carpet microsensors to twenty-four-hour totally monitored TV coverage. Armed men stood guard at the elevators and at the entrance to each stairwell. The bell captain and every bellhop carried sidearms and were required by hotel policy to spend at least six hours a week practice firing in the hotel's downstairs range. All this to protect guests from the politically motivated kidnappers and assassins trailing in the successful, blood-soiled footsteps of groups such as One World United.

The desk clerk, one side of whose hotel blazer had been tailored noticeably fuller in order to accommodate a shoulder holster, took Saul's name and passport, and punched the information into his Interpol com hookup. After several minutes a green light flashed on atop the terminal, thereby declaring Saul free of known terrorist associations and thusly fit to enter the hotel's inner sanctum. The desk clerk rang for a bellhop whose function was to insure that Saul went directly to his destination. The bellhop would stand by outside the door until Saul had finished, and then escort him out.

Saul pressed the buzzer and Michelle, who had been informed of his arrival by the desk clerk, admitted him to her suite. The suite was done up in the popular, eclectic style referred to as Bridge Multicultural. The entry hall, living room, and kitchenette looked, respectively, like they had been assembled from out of the spare parts of a Chinese temple, a New England farmhouse, and a western saloon.

Michelle complimented the rather chaotic decor perfectly. She wore a baggy, three-piece suit, threadbare at the knees and elbows. What fashion designers hailed as poverty chic. Although she had paid nearly $800 for her outfit, Saul suspected she could have found something identical in a used-clothes barrel at the Salvation Army. If she could ever lower herself to go there. Or if she even knew such places existed.

"What have you been up to, love?" she asked Saul. "You look positively horrid."

He tried to give her a flip rejoinder, but, to his horror, suddenly found himself incapable of speech. His tongue refused to move. Then the room began to spin. He toppled forward, and his knees caved out from under him. Michelle reached him just as his head hit the floor.

Acid drops of despair etched deeply intaglioed horrors into the softness of his mind. He dreamed of wires stuffed with cylindrical clocks counting out the cylindrical lifetimes of cylindrical people. And nowhere could he find the slightest outcropping of hope. He had become an antihero, trapped inside a fairy tale without a happy ending, a place where nobody lived happily ever after.

He opened his eyes.

He was laid out in bed. He knew almost at once it belonged to Michelle. Her scent, five hundred dollars an ounce at the finest Paris perfumeries, baited the pillowslips, bidding the stray, unsuspecting male to lay down his head upon her feather-baited guillotine.

"I don't believe it," said Michelle from the open doorway. "That doctor pumped enough sedatives into your hide to keep you asleep for a week."

By propping himself up on one elbow, Saul raised himself into a semisitting position. "What happened? How long have I been out?"

Michelle placed the back of her hand against his forehead. "Lie back down. You're still running a temperature."

"Skip the Florence Nightingale routine. You couldn't diagnose a fever even if your patient had smoke coming out of his ears."

Michelle moved her hand down and tweaked his cheek. "A pity doctors don't prescribe bleeding anymore."

"Medical opinions aside, you didn't answer my question. What happened to me?"

Michelle lit a cigarette. "You collapsed in my doorway about three hours ago. The hotel doctor nearly choked when I told him how many bridge trips you've taken within the past few days. He said that was pretty obviously the problem. You're reacting to the recovery drug. According to him, another dose could bring on cardiac arrest. He said for you to stay in bed, get plenty of sleep, and let your body recuperate."

Saul came to a full, upright sitting position, then hesitated, gathering his strength for an attempt to stand. "I can't do that. Not with Galina Rosmanov still trapped in the wires."

Michelle pointed to the phone. "Look. I'll have Ralph set up a full communications console. You'll be able to talk to anybody you want to, anywhere, from right here in this room."

Saul put his legs over the side of the bed, but couldn't steady them enough to stand up. "It's not the same as eyeball to eyeball. People are less likely to lie with a fist in their face."

"You must have been a great cop."

"One of the best." He clenched his hand and bent his arm at the elbow. "I still hold the Cincinnati P.D. single-season record for most thugs batted in." Unable to stand, he flopped back down prone. "Tell you what. You give me honest answers to a few questions, and I'll do what you say. I'll stay here in bed and rest up."

"No deal. That was the doctor's suggestion, not mine. I promised him I'd convey the message. Which I've done. As far as I'm concerned, henceforth you're on your own. You want to go out and kill yourself, that's your business. I didn't take you to raise."

"And here I had you pegged for a closet Samaritan."

"Looks like your deductive powers aren't as infallible as you'd like us to believe." She sat down beside the bed. "I suppose, though, that you'll keep making life miserable for me until I submit, so, if you came here to grill me, then grill me and let's be done with it."

"Fine." He nudged the nightlight so it shined into her eyes. "Would you reach in my coat there and hand me my rubber hose?"

She permitted herself the faintest trace of a smile as she flicked off the light. "No need for that. I'll have room service send you up a bedpan."

He chuckled. "My, but you do have a knack for taking the jollies out of police brutality." He propped himself up against the bed's headboard. "Actually, it's not going to be all that bad. I've only got one question, really. I'd simply like to know what you and Galina Rosmanov discussed those twenty-odd times she visited you at your Washington office."

Her face went totally blank. "What do you mean," she said, "when she visited me in Washington? I've never met that girl in my life."

"An eyewitness saw her enter your office," Saul lied.

Michelle's mouth curled once again into a faint smile. "You should tell your eyewitness to invest his payoff money in a set of eyeglasses. That girl has never come anywhere near my office."

"But she has been to Bridge Authority Headquarters."

"So what? So have ten thousand other people, this month alone. Maybe she came to buy a ticket or to lodge a complaint against a wirecap or to put in a claim for lost baggage or to visit our museum. I mean what could she and I possibly have to talk about?"

Saul leaned his head back and stared up at the ceiling. "For openers, there's the portable wireless bridge."

Michelle ingested a lungful of air and pumped it back out chock full of indignation. "Get off it, will you? We already settled that."

"Looks like we'll just have to give it another airing, then." He rolled over to face her. "Herman Lindstrom has actually developed a portable wireless bridge. He built two transportals, one of which went inside the wires with Galina Rosmanov."

"I don't believe it." She elongated each word but still couldn't stretch them out far enough to totally cover the shafts of doubt spiking through her confidence. "He couldn't have done it. We watched him too closely."

"Maybe it's *your* spies who need the eyeglasses."

Words oozed out of her mouth like blood from an open wound.

"I'm sure I needn't ask you to fill me in on just how I fit into this scenario."

"Be my pleasure." He brought his feet up under his buttocks like a high jumper preparing to vault over the moon. "I suspect Galina Rosmanov came to you, told you she had a portable wireless bridge, showed you a movie to prove it, then offered to sell it to you."

Michelle lit a cigarette, even though she still had one smoldering in the bedside ashtray. Her hard-boiled reply came out, at best, only mildly poached. "You know, Saul, written up with some good characterization that just might make the New York *Times* best-seller list. In the fiction category, of course. Tell me, what happens next?"

"She sold you one transportal and kept the other. You found out later she planned to sell it to someone else. So you fed something into it just as she entered the wires. That took her off, and gave you a big, fat exclusive."

Michelle smiled, naturally, easily, and Saul knew he had trouble. "Great theory, Saul. Only one logical oversight, albeit a whopper. Suppose, as you say, she was negotiating with us. Wouldn't you suppose, since she was on her way to *Washington,* that the transportal she had in her luggage was the one intended for *us?* And, by extension, wouldn't that lead you to believe she had already delivered the other one to somebody else first? And that they were the ones who got to her?"

"That doesn't hold water, and you know it. It's as easy to bridge to Paris as it is to walk across the street. You could have arranged to pick that transportal up anyplace."

"But so could just about anybody else." Michelle poked him in the chest with her finger hard enough to leave tiny half-moon-shaped nail marks in his skin. "Pack it in, Saul. This affair's like an onion. Peel back one layer and underneath you find another, every bit as acidic. Sure, in time, you might skin it to the core, but all you'll get for your troubles will be a face full of tears."

Saul picked up the bedside room-service call buzzer and bounced it in his palm. "Had I known you were such a philosopher, I would have rung for a cracker barrel and Franklin stove." He returned the buzzer to the nightstand, leaned back on the pillows, and locked his hands behind his head. "I'm not going to back off, Michelle. I'm going to find out who put that girl in there, and I'm going to find out why."

She snubbed out her cigarette with such viciousness that, instead of mashing, it burst. "You do that, Saul. You go right ahead and play supersleuth. To hell with the consequences. Who cares what becomes of the world, so long as Saul Lukas proves once again that he's still the last of the great crusaders."

Her bedside phone rang. She picked it up, listened for a moment, then passed the instrument to Saul. "For you. The New York lab."

"Lukas," he said.

"Saul, Harry Kile here. From New York. I think we've finally got a fix on that second drug you brought us." Saul heard pages rattling as Kile consulted his written notes. "It's a synthetic, like the transference recovery drug you brought in, but this one's on the opposite end of the spectrum. Rather than acting as a stimulant, it acts as a rather powerful depressant. So powerful, in fact, that we could probably label it a poison."

A poison? What could Galina Rosmanov have wanted with a poison? "How does it work?"

"Depends on the dosage, the victim's body weight, age, physical condition, activity level, a whole host of things, but, in general, I would expect to see a loss of feeling in the extremities, a marked lessening of mental faculties, and an inability to accomplish simple mechanical functions such as sitting and walking."

Could it be? Kile had just described Herman's symptoms to the last detail. "And after that?"

Kile flipped to his final page. "Paralysis of the extremities, paralysis of the internal organs. Death."

Death? No. Galina Rosmanov wouldn't have poisoned her lover. She couldn't be that callous. Could she? "What's the antidote?"

"Beats me. I'm not even sure there is one."

Saul gripped the phone so tightly his knuckles whitened. "How long would it take you to find out?"

"Hard to tell. If everything went well, and we didn't run into any unforeseen difficulties, six to eight weeks."

"And how long would you guess someone who had taken this drug could last? The very maximum?"

"As I said, that depends on dosage levels, physical condition, a number of variables."

Damn! Couldn't scientists ever deliver a simple, straightforward answer? Did they always have to intersperse protective layers of probabilities and qualifiers? "Give me a range, then. Minimum to maximum time somebody who had taken that drug could live."

"A range?" Kile considered for several seconds. "My best guess would be four to five days."

Four to five days. Galina Rosmanov had been in the wires for nearly three days already. That meant Herman could theoretically go anytime. "Doc, I have a man who's taken that drug. He needs the antidote, and he needs it today, tomorrow at the latest."

It could have been a crackle in the line, or it could have been Kile chuckling. "I'll get to work on it immediately, but I really can't promise anything. This sort of thing takes time."

Time. The one commodity Saul didn't have and couldn't buy. "Do your best." He hung up the phone.

Struggling against his wooziness, Saul climbed out of bed and began dressing.

"And just where do you think you're going?" asked Michelle.

"I've got to get out to the collector station." He explained the lab's report and its implications. "I've got to see Herman."

"I'm going with you," she said, slipping on her coat. "This has all the potential of developing into a first-rate scandal."

Saul couldn't believe her one-sided, callous outlook. "You mean you want to be around when Herman keels over so you can whisk him under the carpet before word gets out?"

"Don't be flip. Naturally I'm concerned for Lindstrom's health. But if he does die, I want to make sure that the Bridge Authority is in no way held responsible."

Escorted by the hotel bellhop, still standing by outside, they walked down the hall to the elevator.

"You know, sweetheart," said Saul, "I have a hunch that a hundred years from now some industrial organization is going to petition the church to canonize you. Saint Michelle of the Hardened Heart. Patron of money grubbers everywhere."

She didn't argue because, deep down, she half suspected he might be right.

CHAPTER 18

The land whisked by below, a flat, abstractly beautiful pattern of lights and darks. Lush green jungle blending into arid semidesert and slate-gray rock. Saul laid his head against the helicopter's high-backed, foam-padded safety seat, and closed his eyes. Once all travel had been this way. A time for relaxation, observation, and thought. How many times had he sat through his grandmother's fond recounting of her silver anniversary cruise to the Old Country? Each meal remembered in almost impossible detail. Her hands miming the gentle lullaby of the waves. The heightening anticipation of arrival. Dusty remnants of an extinct era. Nowadays hardly anyone rode the sea anymore. Instead everyone rode ten miles under it. Granted, they reached their destination in a fraction of the time they used to, but what they gained in hours, they lost in memories. A curious theft, since few even realized the value or the joy of what had been stolen from them.

The pilot circled in and set his craft down neatly in the center of the concrete landing pad near the station's front entrance. An intercomplex tram collected Saul and Michelle and transported them to the main facility.

Herman had been deemed too ill to be bridged out, so the equivalent of a small hospital had been bridged in. There were so many medical specialists and so much diagnostic equipment crammed into the station's tiny sick bay that Saul had trouble spotting the patient.

When he did, he was aghast. Herman looked terrible, a hundred times worse than when Saul had seen him last. Shriveled lips laid back to the gumline, yellowing teeth, a blackened tongue, great clumps of hair missing. Had Saul not known better, he would have sworn this man lying in front of him was at least ninety years old.

Herman saw Saul, and gave him a feeble wave. "Got a great medical mystery going here, folks," he said weakly. "There's talk about making me the centerfold in next month's *Medical Digest*."

Saul sat down beside him. "How you feeling?" he asked, forcing the words past the constriction in his throat.

"Like a newborn babe in an incubator, what with everybody hustling around trying to pretend I'm not as bad off as they're making me out to be." Herman's horribly sunken, whitening eyes would have easily doubled the pencil sales of a street corner blind man. "I can tell from your face. You know what I've got, don't you?"

Wordlessly, Saul nodded.

Herman responded with the doomed bravado of a small-town sheriff facing the fastest gun in the West. "Well, would you mind sharing the secret with me? After all, I do have a personal interest."

Saul flipped out a cigarette, put it into his mouth, and let it float there like a channel marker on the stream of his conversation. "When was the last time you saw Galina Rosmanov?"

"What has that got to do with it?" Herman attempted to smile, a gesture that only served to enhance his already considerable resemblance to a badly preserved cadaver. "She infect me with the Moscow measles or something?"

Each of Saul's words revolved into place slowly, lethal slugs in the cylinder of a weapon pressed against a heart. "When was the last time you saw Galina Rosmanov?"

Herman wound the end of his sheet into a tight strand and stretched it between his hands in preparation for the garroting of his fondest memories. "The day before she vanished. We met at this chalet in Switzerland. Froehliche's I think was the name of it. Why?"

"Did she cook you anything while you were there? Or mix you a drink?"

Herman began to get the drift. "You think Galina poisoned me. That's what you think, isn't it? Well, you're wrong. I mean, you don't poison someone you love."

Saul couldn't agree more, although he didn't say it. "Just answer my question. Did she make you anything to eat or drink?"

Herman dropped his head to his chest, but didn't have the strength to complete the nod by raising it again. "Yes, she made me something. Something to eat, some exotic Chinese thing. Very spicy, as I recall. Gave me a tremendous case of heartburn. But I've never heard of anyone dying from terminal heartburn."

"But people have been sliced to death by the tip of an iceburg." Saul forced himself to gaze into the glazed porcelain marbles masquerading as Herman's eyes. "I found some drugs in Galina's apartment. You know anything about them?"

"Sure. The instant recovery stuff. I already told you about that."

"No, something else. In addition to that. This one was a poison."

"And you think she gave it to me?"

"That's how it looks."

Herman resisted that conclusion, like an art collector whose prized masterpiece has just been relabeled a fake. "But Saul, she loved me."

Saul finally lit his cigarette. The smoke settled comfortably into his lungs like the final curtain of a very familiar play. "Looks like she might have loved money a little more."

"She sold me out?" An extremely difficult concept for Herman to grasp. Herman toiled for knowledge, not money. He often forgot to cash his paychecks, and he never counted his change. He couldn't conceive of anyone cultivating a personal relationship only in the hope of gaining from it financially. He might have been less naïve had he spent less time in the lab, and more in the world of business.

"I think she was working for the Russians, Herman. Acting as a go-between. They gave her money, and she passed it on to you to fund your research. After you'd succeeded, my guess is she had orders to knock you off so you couldn't duplicate your efforts later for the Bridge Authority. That's where the poison came in. Then she was to have turned the portable wireless bridges over to her comrades. But she pulled a double cross, grabbed off the two units for herself and sold them."

"But the Russians were bound to find out once portable wireless bridges started popping up everywhere. What would happen to her then?"

"I suspect she gambled that once portable wireless bridges went into general use the entire concept of national boundaries would become meaningless. There would be no more Russia, per se, and she wouldn't have to worry."

"That's absurd. Even if Russia ceased to exist as an entity, there would still be individuals who would want retaliation for such a betrayal."

Saul chuckled. "I said she was a spy. I never said she was a good spy. She doused herself in intrigue the way other girls her age drench themselves in perfume, without any understanding of the subtleties involved. She had the right physical requirements for the espionage racket. Contacts and the heartlessness to betray trusts. But she lacked the flinty shrewdness she needed to survive. She was a little girl playing at being Mata Hari. Like any child playing an adult's game she was bound to lose because she didn't fully understand the rules."

"So what happens now? I mean, am I going to die?"

Saul patted his arm. "Let's hope not. I've got the entire Bridge Authority drug lab working on an antidote." Saul put on his most confident expression. "They tell me it will be a piece of cake. By this time day after tomorrow you'll be your normal, ugly old self."

But Herman had seen too many phony expressions of confidence lately to be fooled, even by an expert. "Saul, I . . . I . . ." He couldn't finish. He swung his face around and buried it into his pillow.

Saul sat down on the bed beside him and clasped his shoulder.

"Leave me alone," Herman sobbed. "Just let me be."

"Sure, old buddy. Whatever you want." Saul stood. "Only one more question. Where did you do your work on the military's wireless net?"

Herman rolled over. Tear lines marked both sides of his face. He rubbed them away with the back of his hand, but new ones as quickly replaced them. "What do you want to know that for?"

"Seems to me that if the Bridge Authority had a portable wireless bridge to take apart, that would be a pretty good place to do it. Probably has a foolproof security system already set up, and the necessary scientific gear already in place."

Herman sat up, interested. "Then you think Galina sold one of my units to the Bridge Authority?"

"I'd bet my life on it. Tell me where you did the work."

Herman shrugged. I did most of it at a lab just outside Boulder, Colorado. The Bridge Authority carries it on their docket as the Rocky Mountain Research Facility. Ultra-top-secret place. Like you suspected, it's heavily guarded, completely equipped. But far as I know, they haven't done anything with it since the military net. It's only staffed by a skeleton crew these days. There's nothing going on there."

"At least nothing you know about." Saul gripped the backside of Herman's hand. "You take care. I'll see you again when I get back."

Once outside, Saul leaned against a wall in the computer room. The clock above the computer showed that Galina Rosmanov had less than eight hours remaining. And how many hours did Herman have? In a sudden fit of rage, Saul picked up a nearby pedestal ashtray and flung it at the clock, hitting it squarely, shattering the main panel of LEDs.

He sank back against the wall, tears forming in his eyes. Only Rosie had the courage to approach him. She put an arm around his shoulder and held him to her.

"You hear about Herman?" he asked.

"I didn't have to hear. Maybe twelve hours ago I started to sense it in his body, like a cancerous growth consuming him. He's not going to make it, Saul. No matter what you do for him. It's gone too far."

Maybe she was right. Maybe he couldn't save Herman. But at least he could still save the project Herman had given his life for. And he could bring Herman's killer to justice. Yes, definitely that. Bring Herman's killer to justice. "Rosie, I've got to bridge to Boulder, Colorado."

This was one of those rare occasions when something took Rosie by complete surprise. "You think that's wise? I heard about your two recent medical run-ins. I was under the impression another trip could kill you."

"Both doctors said it was the recovery drug. So I'm not going to take it. I'm going to try that instant version we found at Galina's place. Maybe it won't affect me as much."

"And maybe it will affect you more."

The possibility had occurred to him. "That's why I want you to come along with me. So there's somebody to finish up if I can't."

"Finish up what?"

"I'll tell you on the way to the bridge."

At the weigh-in station, Saul produced one of the instant recovery tablets he had taken from Galina Rosmanov's apartment. He rolled it gently between his thumb and forefinger, treating it as though it were an explosive device that might, at any moment, blow off the top of his head. He shut his eyes, opened them, put the tablet into his mouth, and swallowed it.

Then he approached the bridge.

He stepped inside, took one last look at the world around him, and felt the universe collapse into a hot, bluish haze.

CHAPTER 19

Saul waved off the hostess rushing into the transportal to support him, and stepped forward under his own power.

He felt fine. No queasiness, no dizziness, wide awake, ready to function. Apparently the instant recovery tablets worked exactly as touted.

He flashed his Bridge Authority I.D. to the technician in charge and had him put through a communications patch to Rosie standing by at the collector station. When she came on, Saul told her to go ahead and take the instant recovery tablet he had left behind for her.

She did. Less than fifteen minutes later, she stood beside him, also fully recovered.

Together, they walked to the nearest phone booth. There Saul punched up the number of the Rocky Mountain Research Facility and handed the phone to Rosie.

"Let me speak to Gordon Christianson," she told the switchboard operator who answered. Before leaving the collector station, she and Saul had swung by personnel for a peek at Rocky Mountain's organizational chart. The chart carried Christianson as the facility's chief scientist.

"Gordon Christianson here," he said.

"Gordon, this is Michelle Warren." Rosie extended her free hand in Saul's direction and crossed her fingers. She could do a credible but not a perfect impersonation of Michelle's voice. If Christianson spotted her for a phony . . .

"I don't know what more I can tell you, ma'am," said Christianson with the overdefensiveness of someone forced by his position to spend a great deal of time apologizing for the failings of others. "We've made almost no progress since your last call. We still can't figure out how the infernal contraption works."

Rosie nodded to Saul and winked. "Perhaps it's time I found myself a chief scientist with a bit more imagination," she said.

"No, I beg of you," Christianson responded. "Just a bit longer. We'll break it eventually. That I guarantee. It's just that for such a relatively compact device it incorporates an almost incredible number of radical technological innovations. But please have patience. We'll reason it out."

Rosie took a deep breath. Here came the dicey part. "I'm afraid I can't wait. I've decided to call in an outside expert. Saul Lukas. He and his assistant, Rosie St. Michaels, will arrive there shortly. I want them given free and open access to the device."

"But ma'am," Christianson said, clearly puzzled, "that directly countermands your earlier order, that under no circumstances is Mr. Lukas to be permitted to enter this facility."

Rosie sharpened her voice to a chisel edge, and drove it under Christianson's thin veneer of resistance. "I changed my mind. You now have my express permission to show Mr. Lukas anything he may wish to see."

"Yes, certainly." The man seemed about to argue, but then backed off, like a jilted lover reluctant to learn from his former betrothed of the inadequacies in his makeup that drove her to abandon him. "When he arrives I'll extend him every consideration."

"You just see to it that you do that. Give me a call, say in six or seven hours, and let me know how it's going." She slammed the phone into its cradle and turned to Saul. "First round to the good guys," she told him, and smiled.

They parked their rented car outside Rocky Mountain's front gate. For all the secrecy that shrouded the place, it had a remarkably open facade. Grounds magnificently landscaped with lush grass and expertly pruned shrubbery. A single rambling building with lots of windows. Brick walkways curling past scores of benches and fountains.

Not a steel bar or an electrified fence in sight. Of course Saul hadn't expected there would be. The best security measures weren't the kind you saw. They were the kind that whistled unseen out of the darkness and dealt with your territorial intrusion by slicing you swiftly in two.

They entered the building. Saul displayed his I.D. to the receptionist at the front desk. She placed a call upstairs.

In less than a minute they were joined by a man wearing slightly scruffy blue jeans, a rumpled flower-print shirt, and scuffed sandals, his normal working clothes. To starchen his image as an administrator, he had, for this occasion, donned a new plaid sport coat, which served only to call even greater attention to the casual attire it was meant to conceal. "Mr. Lukas? How do you do. My name is Gordon Christianson. I'm chief scientist here at Rocky Mountain." His hand transferred a fine layer of perspiration to Saul's. "And you must be Rosie St. Michaels. So good to meet you." He bowed stiffly from the waist, like a tin man with one too few hinges.

"I assume Michelle told you why we've come here," said Saul.

Christianson nodded. "Please Mr. Lukas, if I might make one clarificational comment relative to that. My staff and I have been under a tremendous strain on this one. We've been putting in fourteen- and sixteen-hour days in an effort to crack the secret of that device. We've made tremendous progress, but there's a limit to human endurance. We're drained, emotionally, physically, and intellectually. Given a few days to let our findings percolate, to consolidate our insights, given that, we'll solve your puzzle for you. I guarantee it." Christianson belonged not here in a lab but in an animated cartoon, playing the fourth little pig, the most frivolous of any, the one who tries to keep out the wolf by constructing a house with invisible walls of logic.

Saul put an arm around Christianson's shoulders, joining them together as allies against the vicious enemy sniping at them from behind a walnut-paneled barricade of shortsightedness and inconsideration. "Hey, Gordon. Don't worry about it. I'm on your side. No problem. Take as long as you need. I'm not the corporate hatchetman. I didn't come here to stomp on your toes. I'm here to help. That's all." He flashed the broadest, most convincing smile he could generate.

"Honest?" Christianson reacted as though he had just been informed there was a Santa Claus after all.

"My word on it," said Saul.

"You don't know what a relief it is to hear you say that," said Christianson. "To be quite frank, after I talked to Michelle, I had visions of myself out selling apples on a street corner somewhere."

Saul laughed. "Obviously you don't know Michelle that well. She's not really *that* bad." No, she was far worse, not only capable of forcing him to rely on a street-corner applestand for his livelihood, but of arranging for him to receive only the wormiest and most rotten apples from his suppliers. Saul released his grip and stepped back. "Now, what say we take a peek at the device."

"Of course." Christianson swished a handkerchief across his forehead to clear away the droplets of anxiety clinging there like watery parasites. "If you'll follow me."

Christianson led them into the elevator. He put a coded card into the slot beneath the buttons and a sidewall panel slid away revealing an additional thirty buttons, none of them labeled. Christianson pushed two simultaneously. The doors shut and the elevator glided silently downward. Even though the regular floor indicator above the elevator's door exhibited only one basement level, the elevator continued to descend for nearly a full minute before it stopped.

The door opened into a stark, metal-walled gray room, approximately eight feet square. The room was completely empty. Christianson led them inside, and the elevator door closed behind them, sealing them off. There was no other exit. Innocuous half-inch holes ringed the room at precise intervals on two levels, at shoulder height and just below the ceiling. Gun ports, perhaps. Or gas jets. Christianson inserted his card into a wall slot.

The elevator door slid open. A telescoping walkway now traversed the elevator shaft and permitted entry into the lab area on the other side.

"A nice touch," said Saul as they walked over, "using the elevator shaft as a moat."

Once they were safely across, Christianson pushed a button, the walkway receded, and the doorway to the lab hissed shut. "It certainly does discourage door-to-door salesmen," Christianson said rather raffishly. The proximity of dials, analyzers, and instruments restored in him the sense of order he invariably lost when forced to journey outside this, his normal habitat, to deal with the inconsistent volatilities of his fellow human beings.

Christianson escorted them to a corner workbench. "There it is," he said, pointing to an object about the size and shape of an old-fashioned cathedral radio. Christianson picked it up, unclipped the cables leading to a bank of diagnostic devices rack-mounted along the top of the workbench, and handed the device to Saul.

Saul turned it over in his hands several times, examining it from every angle. It was, as Herman had indicated, certainly simple. Basically nothing more than a single card rack containing sixteen standard-sized edge-connected cards. Each card held several 64-bit microprocessors, a number of read-only memory chips, and a sprinkling of random-access memory packages. A subminiature power supply and a matching voltage stabilizer were bolted to the side. There were several other components, none of which Saul could identify. The top of the device, where it rounded off to form its cathedral shape, was hollow, apparently where payloads were inserted and withdrawn.

"Does it have outer panels?" Saul asked.

"Yes," said Christianson. "We took them off to get better access."

"Could you reinstall them for me, please?" Saul asked.

"Of course." Christianson picked up several pieces of dull metal from a nearby bench, snapped the front panels into place, screwed them down, then did the same with the interlocking side panels. "There you are," he said handing Saul the finished product.

Saul hefted it. Completely assembled it weighed barely eleven kilos. "I'd like to take it to our main research center in New York and examine it there," he said.

Christianson's forehead began, once again, to mass produce dewdrops of anguish. "I'm afraid, Mr. Lukas, that request puts me in a rather awkward position. On the one hand, I have Miss Warren's order to co-operate with you in any way I can. On the other hand, I also have a standing order from her stipulating that under no circumstances is that device to leave this laboratory."

"How stupid of me," said Saul snapping his fingers, "to forget to mention that I brought an authorization with me."

"You did?" said Christianson, quite relieved at the ease with which his predicament was apparently to be resolved. "Well, that certainly simplifies matters. Just let me have a quick peek at it, and we'll be on our way upstairs."

"Of course," said Saul. He reached into his coat pocket, and pulled out a small hard-plastic revolver. Its epoxy bullets packed very little punch or accuracy over distance, and it had an unpleasant tendency to explode after two or three firings, but it cost only three dollars, roughly the price of five ice-cream cones or two beers, and thus was easily within the price range of nine-tenths of the world's population.

For Saul, it had quite a different appeal, though. Because of its plastic construction, it was totally undetectable by conventional security scanning systems. Only a hands-on body frisk would turn it up. He had gambled that Rocky Mountain wouldn't go that far with a visiting dignitary, and he had been right.

He pointed the weapon at Christianson's gut. "I think my line here is, 'Stick 'em up.'"

The color drained out of Christianson's face. He shoved his hands to shoulder level and held them there, as though readying them to take the first nails in this crucifixion of his trust. "I have a wife and three children, Mr. Lukas."

Saul tapped him on the cheek with the gun's barrel. "Then unless you want to contribute one more fatherless family to the world, you'd best co-operate. Clear?"

Christianson nodded, trying hard to generate enough moisture in his mouth to lubricate his suddenly parched throat.

"Let's get going." Saul waved his gun toward the elevator.

Christianson shuffled to the elevator door, inserted his activator card into the slot, and walked with them into the tiny room across the shaft. The door slid shut locking them inside.

"Everything O.K., Mr. Christianson?" asked a voice from somewhere on the other side of the wall.

Rosie tightened her grip on the portable wireless bridge. Saul pressed the gun through his pocket against Christianson's spine.

"Yes, Harry," Christianson said with remarkable calm. "Everything's just fine."

"Reason I asked was because you don't look so hot."

"I've been sick. A touch of the flu. I think I'm over the worst of it, though."

"Take care of yourself," said the voice just as the door slid open exposing the elevator.

They rode to the main floor and then walked to Christianson's office. There, Saul had Rosie collect several lamp cords, which he used to secure Christianson to his chair. Saul ripped a swatch from out of one of the linen drapes, knotted it, and stuffed it into Christianson's mouth.

Saul and Rosie then went out to their rented car, locked the portable wireless bridge into the trunk, and drove off.

Saul flashed his priority travel badge, and circumvented the line of people waiting to board the Mexico/South America Bridge.

"When you get to my place," he told Rosie, "have my houseboy put the bridge in my storage vault. Tell him to disengage the combination lock and set the vault to open at my touch only. It's precoded for it. Then you join me at the collector station. Any questions?"

"Only one. How did a nice, genteel, God-fearing lady like me ever get mixed up in an illegal shenanigan like this? And what happens if I get caught?"

Saul kissed her on the cheek. "Plead senility and wear a shawl to court. Not a jury in the world would convict you."

Laughing, she entered the transportal and disappeared.

Saul pulled out another of the instant recovery drugs, put it on the edge of his tongue, swallowed it, and, somewhat reluctantly, walked into the transportal after her.

CHAPTER 20

Saul arrived at the collector station, stepped out of the transportal, and nearly doubled over with pain. So much for the prophylactic effects of the instant recovery tablets. His awaiting hostess maneuvered him into one of the wheelchairs used to transport passengers from arrival to recovery. He showed her his Bridge Authority I.D. and commanded her to push him not to recovery, but to the station director's office, instead.

He had her stop the wheelchair outside the door. He would not be rolled into Michelle's presence like a helpless invalid. He would walk in like a man, no matter how great the pain.

And the pain was very great, indeed. Each of the two steps to the door brought with it a stomach cramp so intense it nearly took his breath away. He inhaled deeply to regain his composure, twisted the door handle, and walked into the office without knocking.

When Michelle saw him in the doorway, her eyes pinched into narrow slits, and her mouth dwindled to a slender line. Given a rope and a rubber stamp bearing the verdict "guilty *in absentia*," she would have been the definitive portrait of a hanging judge.

"Call off the search," she said to whomever she had been talking to on the phone when Saul walked in. "Lukas just turned up."

She slammed the phone into its cradle, came around to Saul's side of the desk, and poked him in the chest with her index finger. "If it isn't the champion of the underdog. The caped crusader himself. I hope you realize, superhero, that your grandstanding cost Christianson his job." Her words came out with the slow, pumping force of a bulldozer shoving dirt over the innocent victims of a massacre. "Worse. You cost him his career. I'm going to personally see to it that he never works in the matter-transmission field again. And unless you want to wind up the same way, you'd better give me back my portable bridge." She held out her hand, as though she suspected he had the device concealed somewhere on his body.

Saul ambled over to a nearby easy chair, moving slowly in a futile effort to lessen his agony. He dropped into the chair and threw one leg casually over the arm. That seemed to help somewhat. He drew back his lips into a wolfish grin. "Seems to me, sweetheart, that you aren't the one with the stick. Seems to me the only question we have to settle here is how high do you have to bid to gain my concession. This go-round you deal with me on my terms, or first thing tomorrow morning I deliver the portable wireless bridge to Mary Hemke."

Michelle returned to her desk, sank into her chair, picked up a pencil, and tapped it rapidly on her desktop, like the radiotelegraph operator on a sinking ship squeezing out one last SOS before scurrying for a lifeboat. "And exactly what is it you're after?"

Saul planted both feet on the floor, like an uprooted weed trying to sink new roots before it withered and died. "For starters, some straight answers. When and how did you find out about the portable wireless bridge?"

Michelle rubbed a hand down the side of her face, as though peeling away a rubber mask. "We knew about it almost from the start. We routinely intercept all communiqués transmitted into and out of the Department of Transportation in Moscow, and that was Galina Rosmanov's contact point. When we found out what they were up to, our initial impulse was to step in and stop them immediately. But then, after giving the situation a bit more thought, we decided that if the Russians wanted to spring the hundred million dollars we estimated it would take to develop a portable wireless bridge, let them. We figured that if Lindstrom actually succeeded, we could always intervene before the Russians took possession of the finished product. So we had everything to gain, and nothing to lose."

Michelle hefted the station director's paperweight, a molded plastic model of a transportal, typical of the gifts the Bridge Authority bestowed upon its employees. The paperweight had been mass-produced in a fully automated plant at a unit cost of less than twenty-three cents. The inscription, two lines commemorating the director's fifteen years of company service, had been put there by a computerized engraving tool hooked into the personnel department's Awards and Mementos Branch. The model had been boxed and address-labeled by a packing machine. The day the station director removed the model from its shipping container marked the first time any human being had touched it.

"When we learned that Herman had succeeded, we tried to get him to turn the devices over to us. But he denied that they even existed. We next attempted to steal them, but he had them too carefully hidden. So, as a last resort, I had Ralph Ferguson approach Galina Rosmanov with a deal. He offered, on our behalf, to pay her two million dollars for the two completed units. But she wouldn't go for it. She insisted on retaining one for her government. So we settled on two million for the other. Even at that we considered it a bargain. Less than two one-hundredths what we would have had to pay to develop it ourselves. We gave her the money, and she gave us the bridge."

Michelle categorized what came next with the hardened shamelessness of an unrepentant sinner, eager to confess her transgressions, hear the conditions of her absolution, and hasten forth into the world to sin anew. "We knew she would turn the second prototype over to the Russians soon thereafter. Naturally, we couldn't let that happen. If the Russians ever got hold of that portable wireless bridge, they would use it to smuggle agents into every major American city."

"And I suppose the United States government wouldn't have done the same thing to the Russians?"

The edges of Michelle's lips curled slightly upward into a miniature smile. "Naturally, but with far higher ideals. In any event, since we could not let the Russians have the device, we took steps to prevent it."

"And those steps included feeding something into Galina's portable wireless bridge just as she entered a conventional bridge."

Michelle pressed her left and right fingertips together and made a cage with her hands to demonstrate how easily one could form a trap for the unwary. "Yes. We tied into transmission control, waited until we got a notification of impending transmittal, and then zapped her." She smacked her palms together.

Galina Rosmanov could make medical history, here. The first person to die from a confirmed hemorrhaging of corporate morality. "You picked a pretty complex method of assassination."

"My sentiments exactly, especially since there was a great deal of conjecture among my technical staff as to actually what would happen. Theories ranged all the way from nothing to a small-scale nuclear explosion. In the end we decided to do it this way more or less as a test."

"Even though you risked losing the second portable bridge?"

"Sure. Why not? We didn't need it. We already had one to dissect and study. Failing there, we still had Herman as a last resort."

"One thing bothers me. After deciding to go that route, why call me in? Why not just let her dissipate inside the wires?"

"That would have been too obvious. She was an international celebrity, remember. We did have to put up a front. It seemed a fair exchange. A few public relations lumps in trade for the elimination of a major threat to world normalcy."

"That's why you kept pressing me to drop the search. Because you really didn't want her out. But what about the Russian? Nikolei Bulgavin? How did you persuade him to agree to call it off?"

"Quite simple." Michelle displayed the pride of a renowned artist unveiling the latest in a long string of masterpieces, each intricately crafted from strands of intrigue and deceit. "I told him flat out that he didn't have the slightest chance of ever laying hands on a portable wireless bridge. As a sop, in return for his promise not to press for Galina's extrication, I offered to sell him certain proprietary technical information, outmoded from our point of view, which could improve the Russian's conventional wire net considerably."

"And he went along with that?"

"He had no choice. It was table scraps or starvation." Michelle assumed the stoop-shouldered stance of a Sunday orator trundling a soapbox into a park. "You know, Saul, you have a remarkable inclination to ignore the fundamental sociological patterns at work

here. If you don't get your way, you threaten to turn the portable
wireless bridge over to Mary Hemke and One World United. Let's
think about that for a moment. I want to maintain the bridge network as it is. They want to totally alter it by disseminating portable wireless bridges to the world. Both of these goals, at least to
the people holding them, are perfectly justifiable and rational. As
the system is now, people travel on time, in relative safety, at minimal cost. If the system were altered, people would travel on time,
in relative safety, at minimal cost. In other words, there will be
order and essentially the same results no matter which faction
wins out. What frightens me is the transitional period. Years, perhaps decades of bedlam while people learn to adapt to their new
system. I ask you, will that turmoil be worth it to achieve something which, in the end, won't leave us with anything much better
than what we have now?" She put her hands on her desktop and
pushed herself up to a loftier position. "You know when this
whole affair started, we gave serious consideration to the possibility of promoting the portable wireless bridge. Economically, we
would have made a fortune. We would have mass-produced it and
marketed it, developed accessories, set up a maintenance plan.
We'd have made billions. But in this case, I decided there were
priorities greater than money."

Michelle thrust out her chin like the figurehead on a raft of
reason. "Saul, I consider this device to be potentially every bit as
dangerous as the atomic bomb. It must be suppressed. I think the
public at large, if they were adequately informed, would agree."

This was something they had quarreled over often during their
short marriage, Michelle's persistent tendency to make important
decisions on behalf of other people, Saul included.

"Still functioning as national arbiter of the public good, I see."
Saul gave her a slight variation of the argument he had given her
so often before. "Sure, maybe the portable wireless bridge tempo-
rarily turns the world topsy-turvy. But it's not up to you, or to me,
or to the Bridge Authority, or to any other single entity to arbitrarily decide to withhold it. That decision belongs to the people,
and I think they should be given a chance to make it."

Michelle shook her head. "The surface advantages look too
good. Low-cost transportation. Immediate access to anywhere in

the world. That's pretty potent stuff. Given that choice, I have no doubt which way the people will go. But they will be wrong." She wagged her finger like a mystic inscribing scripture on a wall. "That's your biggest failing, Saul. You don't understand the singularly most unpleasant aspect of responsibility. No matter what I do here, I'm going to alter the course of civilization. Either in a negative sense by forcing it to struggle along the way it is, or in a very dynamic sense by turning it completely on its ear. Either way I run the risk of not being able to live with myself ever again because of the nagging doubt that I did the wrong thing. But the point is, I'm prepared to take that chance in the interest of doing something I really feel to be right."

Saul equated her impassioned speech with the beautifully fili-greed gratework covering the entrance to a sewer. "Very flowery, Michelle. Now that you've said your piece, let's discuss how we go about getting Galina Rosmanov out of the wires."

Michelle's hands collapsed to her sides like the struts of a kite torn to bits in a tornado. "Sure. You don't care about anything except for some stupid code of honor that says you always have to finish what you start. Well, there are times when that code doesn't apply. There are times when you have to let things slide for the greater good."

Saul repeated his ultimatum as though it were a magical incantation that would shield him from the enchantress named common sense. "I want Galina Rosmanov. You let her die, and I turn the bridge over to Mary Hemke."

Since defeat seemed inevitable, Michelle turned her attention toward the negotiation of a favorable surrender. "What about the bridge she took into the wires with her?"

"She gets out, and you get that one, too."

"Your word on it?"

"My word."

Before capitulating, Michelle dredged up one final contention. "Saul, this girl has spent longer inside the wires than anyone has ever done on a consecutive basis before. I've discussed it with Dr. Ryker. He's convinced that by now she's been totally altered. The girl who comes out of those wires isn't going to even vaguely resemble the girl who went in. She's going to be a moron, Saul. A vegetable. A freak. Her mental processes will be shot. Ryker's convinced of it. She'll live the rest of her life needing someone to take care of her. She'll be unable to speak or to control her bodily functions. It's far more humane to leave her inside. Let her drift off in peace. Let people, let her fans remember her the way she was."

Even though a vision of the horrors he had witnessed at the Ryker Sanitarium flashed through his mind, still Saul stuck to his hard line. "I want her out, Michelle. As a human being, or as a blob of jelly. I want her out."

"All right. Have it your way." Michelle returned to her chair, sat down, reached into her briefcase, and removed a blue-covered document that she slapped onto the desk in front of her. "This is the monograph logging what we did to her."

Saul reached for it.

"I'll save you the trouble," she said. "We upped Galina Rosmanov's weight by exactly 3.4 kilos. But there's a kicker." Michelle seemed to be having a great deal of difficulty finding the words to express herself. "Remember, we didn't know what effect the additional weight would have, so we didn't want to take any chances. What I mean is, well, the 3.4 kilos. It's not just a block of inert matter or anything like that. It's an object, something that we put in there as insurance in case nothing happened and she came out the other end."

"Insurance? What are you talking about? What exactly did you transmit in there with her?"

Michelle pointed toward the upper regions of space, where the air was pure and visibility unlimited. "You have to view it from our position. Saul, we . . ."

Saul pounded his hand on her desktop. "Enough with the idealistic eyewash, Michelle. Just tell me in simple language what you transported in there with her."

Michelle moved her chair back, away from him, as though terrified that when he heard her response, he would strike her. And she was right. "Five sticks of dynamite, some wiring, and a percussion cap. We transported a bomb in there, Saul. Set to go off the instant she sets foot outside."

CHAPTER 21

A score of doctors and nurses fluttered about Herman's room like white butterflies cross-pollinating the instruments connected to the fifty microsensors imbedded in his body.

Saul threaded his way through to Herman's bed, knelt down beside it, and gently jostled Herman's shoulder. "Hey, buddy. You awake?"

Herman turned his head in Saul's direction. He did not bother to remove the damp cloth covering his eyes. There was no reason to. His eyesight had gone several hours before. He was now totally blind. "Saul? Is that you?" His hand fluttered through the air like a mourning dove searching for sanctuary from the onset of nightfall.

Saul caught his friend's hand and covered it with both of his own. It was like holding the hand of a wax dummy. Or a corpse. "How you feeling?"

"Like a bionic man. They've got me hooked to a kidney machine, a heart/lung machine, and a nerve path machine. I've got so many wires coming out of me I feel like one of those electrical company ads that show twenty-five cords plugged into a single outlet with some caption underneath about the dangers of overloading your circuits." His smile peeled away as though it had been stuck in place with second-rate adhesive. "This a social call, or business?" he asked.

"Business, I'm afraid." Saul moved aside to let a nurse replenish a bottle of fluid seeping into Herman through a tube taped to his neck. "I've got some new input on the Galina Rosmanov thing, and I want your opinion."

Every monitor in the room suddenly showed a startling rally. "I thought you took me off that."

Specialists hurried in to study the readouts in an effort to divine the cause of Herman's sudden upturn.

"I had to replace you, Herman," said Saul. "I had no choice. You were a prime suspect."

"And now I'm not?" The instruments jumped again.

"Now you're not. I came to you because you're the master. You're the man with the answers. You're the one I trust."

The specialists grew increasingly perplexed. Here they were, the finest medical/electrical diagnosticians in the business, yet not one of them could explain the increased life force registered on their monitors.

"After a stroking like that," said Herman, "I'm going to look awfully stupid if it turns out I can't help you. What's the new data?"

"I know how much Galina Rosmanov's weight was upped."

"You do? That's fantastic. We should have no problem whatsoever getting her out. How much was it?"

The specialists consulted each other in a corner of the room.

"Three point four kilos. But that's only the start. You see, the weight was added in the form of a bomb rigged to go off immediately after it pops out of the bridge. Here's my question. Is there any way that we can separate Galina Rosmanov from her luggage before we bring her out?"

Herman thought about that for some time before answering. "It's never been done, but theoretically, a really sharp maintenance man might be able to go in and isolate her. But it would be tricky, with not the slightest guarantee of success."

The specialists finally arrived at a consensus. They attributed Herman's minor upturn to a slight aberration in the power levels of the station's electrical input feeder lines, and returned to the station's cafeteria where they resumed their game of pinochle.

"Got any suggestions on which maintenance man might be able to pull it off?"

"Well, Carl Eller and Judy Laskow are the best I know of. Either one of them might possibly handle it. But there's somebody better, yet."

"Who?"

Herman thumped himself on the chest with the force of someone banging a bass drum to signal the start of a parade. "Me, Saul. Yours truly."

Not often did Saul witness such bravery. A crippled blind man volunteering to confront the source of his darkest nightmares. "You may be right, but do you think you're, well, physically up to it?"

Herman pointed off somewhere over the rainbow. "Saul, in there, I won't need my arms or my legs or my eyes. It's not like that. In there you operate through mental control. You don't need eyes to see; you don't need hands to feel; you don't need legs to walk. And I don't think anybody understands what goes on in there better than I do."

"You really talk a good ball game for somebody who's never even been inside. That's true, isn't it? You never have been inside."

Herman argued his case with the frantic intensity of an innocent man riding toward the gallows atop the shoulders of a lynch mob. "What difference does that make? I'm the one who designed those bridges. I've debriefed probably a thousand maintenance men, and at least twice that many passengers. That should certainly be enough to offset a lack of actual firsthand experience. I can handle it, Saul. Put me inside, and I know I can handle it."

"You could die in there. You realize that."

"In there, out here, what makes the difference? I'm a dead man either way. You know that as well as I do."

In fact Saul had checked with the New York drug lab just before coming to Herman's room, and the researchers there had indeed confirmed his worst fears. Barring an unforeseen breakthrough, they were weeks away from developing an antidote to Galina Rosmanov's poison. Herman would die, very soon, and very painfully.

Saul nodded and rose. "I'll make the arrangements."

A hostess pushed Herman to the transportal in a wheelchair.

One of the maintenance men strapped a maintenance jacket on him and made the adjustments necessary to mold it to his frame. When the maintenance man was satisfied with the fit, he and Saul boosted Herman to his feet and walked him into the transportal.

Since there were no seats inside, they propped him up as comfortably as possible on the floor. The maintenance man withdrew, leaving Saul and Herman alone. "Still time to back out," said Saul.

Herman chuckled. "That's like asking a marshal to dodge the noon-hour gunfight."

Saul withdrew from the transportal and nodded at the technician in charge. The technician keyed the proper data into the transmission computer and turned to Saul for final go-ahead.

Saul glanced into the transportal at Herman. Never had Saul seen a man look so terrified. But then Saul had never attended an execution. He gave the technician the signal to proceed.

The technician punched his send button, and Herman, his hands balled into tight fists, disappeared.

CHAPTER 22

As a precautionary measure just in case Herman failed and the bomb came tumbling out, Saul had the station's maintenance staff surround the transportal with an eight-foot-high wall of sandbags.

After that, there was nothing left to do except wait.

Saul sat down on a large piece of exposed piping, leaning against the wall behind it, bracing his legs against another smaller piece of piping to keep from sliding off.

Michelle drifted over, reached into Saul's inside jacket pocket, and helped herself to one of his cigarettes.

"Sorry I don't have any color co-ordinated to match your outfit," Saul said holding out his lighter.

"These are hard times," she replied leaning over the flame, steadying his hand with both of hers. "We all have to expect to make an occasional sacrifice." Michelle relished a good argument and would often provoke one to relieve the tedium of a long wait. But Saul wasn't in the mood to play. In silence, he put away his lighter, leaned back against the wall and stared laconically up at the ceiling.

Michelle shrugged and drifted off into the crowd in search of a more willing adversary.

Since the sandbags blocked access to the main transportal, the station's engineer had tied an auxiliary unit into a secondary wire. Word had circulated throughout the system that this auxiliary was to be used only for transportation absolutely vital to the mission at hand.

So a great deal of curious commotion swirled through the room when the auxiliary's receiving light went on and Rosie appeared inside. The hubbub grew considerably louder when Rosie, instead of going limp the way passengers were supposed to, walked straight out of the transportal under her own power.

Michelle, recognizing the effects of the instant recovery tablets, scowled across the room at Saul, but said nothing.

Saul jumped up and went to Rosie. "You get everything taken care of?" he asked her.

"Little Miss Efficiency in person," she answered. "The bridge is safely locked away inside your private vault." She took in the apparent lack of activity around her. "What's going on here?"

Saul led her to his pipe and sat down beside her. "I finally found out how much Galina Rosmanov's weight was upped. It turned out to be the Bridge Authority who had done it." He jerked his thumb toward Michelle in the manner of an umpire ejecting a player for grossly unsportsmanlike conduct. "And get this. They added the extra weight in the form of a bomb."

Rosie returned Michelle's malevolent stare with an exaggerated smile and a demure waggle of her fingers. "A regular wolf in Saks Fifth Avenue clothing, that one. So how does Galina get out?"

Saul looked at the sandbagged transportal the way squadron commanders in World War I movies used to gaze forlornly into the sky at the vanishing specks carrying their young charges off to battle the Hun. "Herman volunteered to go in and try separating Galina from her luggage. If he succeeds, we can pop Galina and let the bomb dissipate inside."

"Herman went into the wires? I thought they terrified him."

"They do. But so did the prospect of dying from poison out here. At least this way he gets a shot at pulling off one last technological coup."

Rosie tugged her shawl tighter around her shoulders but couldn't halt the progress of the chill creeping down her spine. "But Saul, Galina Rosmanov is the one who poisoned him. Maybe he plans to fix it so she joins him on his final journey."

Saul shook his head. "I think deep down he still loves her. Despite everything she's done to him, I think he'll do his best to save her."

"How long has he been in?" Rosie asked.

Saul looked at the clock above the transportal control panel. "Nearly two hours. The worst part of it is we have no way of telling what's going on in there. There are no instruments capable of picking up that kind of thing."

"Mind if I give it a shot?"

"Be my guest."

Rosie commandeered one of the room's few chairs and had Saul drag it as close to the transportal as possible. "Could you keep everyone quiet for a while?" she asked as she sat down.

"Sure." Saul announced what Rosie was about to try and asked for silence. Everyone immediately complied, everyone except for Michelle who filled the room with the blustery click of her high-heeled shoes as she stormed out, unwilling to dignify such quackery with her presence.

Rosie closed her eyes, placed her palms to her temples, and let her head slump to her chest. She sat that way for several minutes.

Then she screamed.

Her hands snapped outward and clawed through the air with the fury of a trapped mole digging its way through the rubble of a collapsed burrow. Her mouth snapped open and closed, but no sounds came out. Twin trails of spittle dribbled down either side of her chin. Just as Saul was about to shake her back to consciousness, her frenzied motion slowed to a stop, her arms collapsed to her sides, her face softened and became calm, and she began to speak.

A densely compacted pellet of terror clogged his throat, then slowly metamorphosed into a globule of regenerative ointment that spread throughout his body, healing his afflictions. His hands. He could move them again. And his eyes. They showed him scenes he had never imagined existed. Braided rainbows of electrical energy, trailing through the wires in lovely delicate strands. Great black walls, which he later came to associate with the presence of resistors. Gating impulses in the form of huge floppy disks, which revolved lazily in front of him, sealing off his passage except for the few brief microseconds when he could scoot quickly through their narrow apertures.

Abruptly, he reached a slight discontinuity in the line. A maintenance man would have chalked it off to tolerable error and let it go. It was the type of thing caused by a slight accumulation of interwire debris. Except in this case that debris consisted of slough from Galina Rosmanov and her deadly baggage.

Theoretically, the convoluted path of the discontinuity should lead him inward to the heart of Galina's expanded bulk.

He paused for a moment to double-check the tools in his maintenance belt. The Freon cluster, capable of sucking up ten thousand times its own weight in particulate muck. The mica chips, two 4 by 950s and two 5 by 1000s. The serial arrays. And all the rest.

Satisfied that everything was in good working order, he began his journey inward, crawling hand over hand along a beam that grew fatter and skinnier at irregular intervals as it faded in and out of spec. When the beam finally petered out, he hooked into the Q channel and rode it to a point just beyond its attenuator.

There he collided with a stationary phase shift. In order to pass, he had to remove four klystrons and adjust the timing. He traveled onward without encountering another barrier until he reached a converter-wired PIN diode, which he had to goose open with his field inverter. But that marked the end of his trek. The PIN gated open to reveal the immense shapeless blob that contained Galina Rosmanov.

Herman immediately checked the blob's delta Q and found it extremely feeble. He couldn't risk going in and slicing her out the most obvious way, with a signal diverter. Since the timing input and monolithic amp were both normal, he bypassed the sync amp to see if he could split her off like that.

But nothing happened. In fact her delta Q degraded even more, bringing with it a nasty power leakage. There was apparently only one way to do it. Fine-tune the parametric amplifier, the microwave filters, and the ruby crystals, then disentangle her by hand.

After making the proper adjustments in tuning, he poked a hand gingerly into the crackling mass and groped around in search of the junction charge bonding Galina to her luggage. At elbow depth he penetrated a vague, withering shape. The leakage flared, and his hand went stiff. He gave it a shake in an effort to restore feeling, but instead his hand fell off and disintegrated.

Oddly enough, the loss didn't bother him in the slightest. He calmly stuck his other hand in, and continued to grope the remainder of the way around Galina's form.

With the side of his hand, he nudged away the snarled quadraxial impulses by which Galina was bound. But in doing so he caused another leakage flare which, this time, claimed both his legs.

Still undaunted, he slipped through a multilayer capacitor and disconnected the liquefied feed-throughs thus setting up the final exercises necessary to set Galina free. He misjudged the strength of the output signal though, and paid for it with half of his remaining hand. Working as best he could with only two fingers, he cut back on the accelerating voltage, stabilized the discretion signal, and primed Galina for her exit into the world.

He popped her loose from her luggage, and pushed her outward, but couldn't avoid the pulse ripple trailing her unrestrained mass. It bounced him into the wire's insulating barrier destroying forever what little remained of his body. In the last purely physical gesture he would ever make, he pursed his nonexistent lips and blew one final kiss to Galina.

Then, trapped in the flow of the tertiary carrier beam, he zipped through the safety interlocks like they were so much butter, and headed outward on the most exciting journey of his life. A nonstop flight to the end of infinity.

Rosie raised her head, tears streaming down her cheeks. "He's gone," she said.

Almost simultaneously, Sammy Blonder exclaimed, "He did it! I show two distinct masses in there. Only one trouble." Blonder fiddled with his dials, but his metering devices refused to budge. "The two masses are so garbled, I can't tell which is which."

Saul stood anxiously by while Sammy went through the rather laborious process of vectoring his calibrations. "What happens if you bring out the bomb first?" Saul asked.

Recalibration got Sammy nowhere. In frustration he smacked his palm against his control panel. "We disrupt whatever slender equilibrium is left in there. Whatever remains will start to dissipate and be lost to us forever." Sammy checked his dials again, as though they might suddenly decide to reconsider and give him the answer they had so far concealed. But they remained as hopelessly inscrutable as ever. "I simply can't tell which mass is which."

Saul traced an intricate pattern atop the console, a pattern which ended exactly where it had begun. "Then pick one at random and bring it out," he said with far more stoicism than he felt.

Blonder nodded and turned. In a decidedly unscientific manner he shut his eyes and pushed the first button he touched.

CHAPTER 23

The receive light flickered weakly like some newborn phosphorescent insect struggling for a toehold on life. Each time it brightened, Saul involuntarily braced himself for the shock wave of a bomb.

But none came.

The light gave one more convulsive series of oscillations, flared briefly to full incandescence, then faded to darkness. And still there was no explosion. Whatever they had, it was definitely not the bomb. But was it Galina Rosmanov?

"Is she out?" Saul asked Sammy Blonder.

Blonder's hands skimmed across his control panel, flicking out the splinters of information, which, fitted together, would give him a cogent picture of the whole. When he had it, he turned to Saul and grinned. "She's out."

A cheer swept round the room. Several men headed for the transportal to remove the sandbags.

"No, wait," said Saul. Two memories flashed through his mind. One, the beautiful, graceful Galina Rosmanov he had watched dancing on a movie screen. The other, the hideous, misaligned freak he had witnessed at the Ryker Sanitarium. Suppose, in the final analysis, Michelle turned out to be right? Suppose Galina Rosmanov emerged horribly disfigured? Despite the girl's wickedness, Saul felt a certain obligation to her, the kind a lawyer feels toward a client even though he knows that client to be guilty. No matter what Galina Rosmanov had done, if she did emerge deformed she at least deserved protection from the gross indignity of immediate public exposure. "Sammy, send her on through to my villa. Right now, before anybody sees her."

"What? Why?"

"Never mind why. Just do it."

Blonder shrugged. "You're the boss."

Blonder vectored in the proper co-ordinates, then pushed the button sending Galina, sight unseen, through the wires to Saul's villa.

"Now send me there, too." Saul popped one of the instant recovery tablets into his mouth and stepped into the weigh-in station attached to the auxiliary transportal.

Rosie caught the weigh-in station door on the way shut. "Do you think this is wise?" she asked. "I mean remember what the doctor said about riding wire."

"Don't worry," said Saul. "The instant recovery tablets seem to protect me just fine." He shuddered as he remembered just how big a lie that was.

He blew Rosie a kiss as she shut the door.

Saul had moved from the weigh-in station into the transportal proper when Michelle entered the room. "I have to talk to him," she told Sammy. "In private."

Blonder passed her the intercom headset and cut in the hush circuit so she and Saul could converse without being overheard.

"Saul." Her voice crackled like a string of firecrackers, each succeeding word exploding out of the intercom with a blast of fury. "What are you trying to pull? Why didn't you contact me when she came out? I got it secondhand from one of the standby engineers. And why did you ship her off to your villa? And where is the second portable bridge?"

Saul looked out at his former wife through the quartz glass safety door. "You know, sweetheart, you asked every conceivable question except for one. How is Galina Rosmanov? But then I tend to forget that when it comes to hero worship your biggie isn't Albert Schweitzer but rather Attila the Hun."

She shouted so loudly into her headset that her voice penetrated the hush circuit and became clearly audible to everyone in the room. "Enough with the sarcasm. You give me a straight answer and you give it to me now. Did you or did you not retrieve the second device?"

Saul saw no point in antagonizing her further. "I did not."

"Where is it, then?"

"Still inside the wires."

"Well, when do you plan to bring it out?"

"I don't. According to Sammy Blonder, it started to dissipate the minute we brought out Galina Rosmanov."

"You mean I'll never get it?"

"Correct. But neither will anybody else."

As Saul suspected, Michelle readily accepted that as a suitable outcome. She didn't really care what shape the puzzle took so long as she wound up in sole possession of every available piece. "Then what about the other device? Remember, we did have a bargain. I gave you the weight of the bomb, you promised me the other device."

Saul extended his hand to eye level. "Isn't this where you're supposed to unfurl a contract signed in blood?"

Ignoring regulations, Michelle stormed through the weigh-in station, gripped the transportal entry door and yanked it, but once a passenger was sealed inside, only the transportal engineer, Sammy Blonder in this case, could open it. Sammy looked to Saul, and Saul shook his head, so the door remained firmly locked.

"Saul," Michelle said, speaking so loudly she once again breeched the hush circuit, "you promised me the portable wireless bridge. I acted in good faith, now I demand that you fulfill your end of the bargain."

In actuality, Saul had never intended to do anything but. He had gotten what he wanted, Galina Rosmanov free of the wires. Plus, he had given his word. "I'll send you the device by wire."

"No." Michelle double-checked to make sure the hush circuit was completely up. She certainly did not want anyone to hear the director of the Bridge Authority making the statement that came next. "Don't put it into the wires. Whatever you do, don't put it into the wires. It's far too valuable. I can't take the slightest risk with it. Tell me where it is, and I'll send a plane."

"However you want it. It's at my villa."

"I'll charter something immediately." She yanked off the headset, handed it to Blonder, and left the room.

Saul turned, nodded to Sammy, and braced himself against the transportal's back wall.

Sammy pressed the button marked "Send."

An incredible blade of pain sliced through Saul's body. He screamed out at Blonder to abort the transmission, but his plea came too late, the transmission process was too far along. In his last instant of consciousness, he conceded that he had finally pushed his luck too far. But at least there was one bright spot. At least he wouldn't live long enough to regret it.

He materialized, screaming, at the other end, every nerve ending in his body afire. He could barely breath. His heart beat at three times normal speed. How long did he have? How long could a human being tolerate such pain? Five minutes? Ten? His houseboy dragged him out of the transportal and carried him to the living-room sofa. "I will phone for a doctor," his houseboy said heading for the foyer.

"No." Saul called him back. It's too late." Another wave of pain hit him, one which would easily have killed a lesser man. "The girl. Galina Rosmanov. Is she here?"

The houseboy nodded. "She is, but sir, she is very . . ." His English was not good enough to adequately express his meaning. "She is not like a regular person. She is very different."

Saul remembered Michelle's warning that the girl would be horribly disfigured. "I must see her. And quickly. I don't have much time."

"When I left her she was asleep. Recuperating, I think, from her voyage through the wires."

Of course. Even under normal conditions she would have to rest for at least an hour after emerging. Hard to tell how long she would be out after the prolonged stay she had experienced.

"Carry her down. Awake or asleep, however. I must see her."

"As you wish." The houseboy stood, and headed for the stairs.

Saul opened his mouth and sucked in air, but it seemed to have become a foreign element to him, something his lungs could no longer assimilate. It burned the whole way down his throat and filled the back of his mouth with the rancid taste of blood.

His houseboy re-entered the room. Alone.

"Where is she?" Saul asked, having to marshal up every remaining ounce of strength to get those few words out.

Wordlessly, his houseboy pointed toward the open doorway.

And Galina Rosmanov walked in.

To all appearances she looked completely normal. In fact she looked better than normal. Her skin glowed. Her eyes sparkled. She resembled someone newly returned from an extended stay at a very exclusive health spa. She had traded her heavy winter clothes for one of Saul's shirts. Its ragged collar and frayed sleeves only served to underscore the incredible perfection of the girl wearing it. Saul had known many attractive women in his life, but never one so radiantly beautiful as this. She had not a single physical flaw, not even so much as a blemish. Incredible as it seemed, rather than coming out of the wires malformed, she had emerged looking even better than she had before she went in.

"I understand I owe you my life," she said. She spoke in flawless English, which Saul thought rather odd considering that her publicity file specified she spoke only Russian. He started to ask her about it when a horrible seizure of pain contorted his body and robbed him of the ability to speak.

"Oh, you're ill," Galina said hurrying to him. She knelt down beside him and placed her hand on his forehead. "You have a terrible fever." She moved her hand to his chest. "And your heart feels ready to burst."

"Get . . . get me a doctor," Saul gasped, sorry now that he hadn't let his houseboy do so earlier, when a doctor still might have been able to do him some good.

"I don't think that will be necessary," Galina said with the inscrutable smile typical of church madonnas and homicidal maniacs.

She crawled onto the sofa beside Saul, and pressed her thinly clad body to his.

His strength was completely gone. He could do nothing to ward her off. He could only lay there beside her and passively allow her, the woman who had murdered his best friend, to work her deviltry on him.

She placed one hand on either side of his head, and let her

fingertips gently caress his temples. She moved her mouth over his. And kissed him.

He awoke alone in his bedroom. And he felt fine. Completely restored, both physically and psychologically. But why? By all rights, instead of being king of the hill, he should be six feet under it. Spontaneous recovery? No, that kind of thing happened only on the afternoon soaps, never in real life. Perhaps a doctor had paid him a visit while he slept. But he saw no evidence of that, either. No pill bottles beside his bed. No needle punctures on his body.

No, there had been only Galina, and her strange kiss, devoid of passion, yet filled with love.

He swung his feet to the floor and gingerly stood, clinging to the bedpost for support since he had no idea if he was really as healthy as he felt. Apparently so. Not only was he able to stand unsupported, he had a crazy urge to slip on his sweat suit and take his normal three-kilometer jog around the boundaries of his estate.

"I'm glad you're feeling better," said Galina from behind him.

From where he stood he faced the only entrance to the room, and he could have sworn she hadn't come through it. But then he had been rather preoccupied with his own well-being, and could, conceivably have glanced away at the crucial instant. After all, how else could she have entered? His room was on the third story, so she couldn't have come in the window. Unless she could sprout wings. He chuckled to himself. Or walk through walls. "Much better, thank you. Although I'm not quite sure why."

Galina sat down in the overstuffed chair beside his bed, pulled her knees to her chest, and encircled them with her arms, as if guarding the delicate porcelain quality of her skin against the danger of an inadvertent chip. "Call it a miracle," she said. "You do believe in miracles, don't you?"

"Sure. But in my league, a miracle is when you pick up a pair of dice with a dollar in your pocket and set them down owning the casino."

Her laugh sparkled through the room like tiny bubbles of childhood and was contagious enough to force Saul to join in.

He sat down on the bed beside her chair and studied her. She didn't fit his preconceived notion in the slightest. Here she was, barely a woman, a Soviet agent, a murderess. Yet she had an aura of kindliness and wisdom about her one would expect to find only in someone who had spent a very long lifetime sitting cross-legged atop a Tibetan mountain. That quality, coupled with her soft, fragile femininity, had a devastating effect upon Saul. He wanted badly to reach across and touch her, but not because he felt drawn to her romantically. Rather because she attracted him the way a powerful religion attracts a prodigal sinner with the promise of renewed self-respect.

As though sensing his desire, and his accompanying reluctance to fulfill it, she took the initiative, reached across to the bed, and laid the back of her hand on his cheek. A pleasant warmth radiated outward from the point of contact through his entire body. "You're feeling better." She spoke it as a statement, not a question.

"Much. Do I have you to thank for that?"

"No. The seed of rejuvenation lies dormant within everyone. You healed yourself. I merely acted as the trigger."

As he sat there close to her, Saul noticed something quite strange. The movement of her lips did not quite coincide with the sounds emerging from her mouth, as though her voice were being dubbed in one language while she spoke in another. "You know, Galina, we were worried that you would pop out of the wires radically altered by the experience. Apparently we were right, but not in the negative sense we expected. You're certainly different, but the change seems to have been a positive one. Do you have any idea what happened to you in there?"

Galina twisted around so she could face him, putting her back against one arm of the chair, her toes against the other. She rested her chin on her knees, and spoke in her odd, unsynchronized way. "No idea whatsoever. I'm a total blank from the time I stepped into the transportal in Mexico City until I stepped out of it here."

"And thus far you've experienced no adverse effects?"

"Only a strong tendency to tire rather easily. In fact, if you wouldn't mind, I would like to go to my room for a short nap right now."

"Of course. When you wake up I'll have my cook prepare us something to eat."

"That would be quite nice." In getting up, she laid her hand on his knee, sending another tingle through his body. "And, once again, thank you."

Saul stood up to escort her to her room, but she shook her head. "Don't bother. I can find my own way. We'll talk more once I wake up."

"I'll look forward to it."

With that, she smiled at him, waved good-by, and vanished into thin air.

CHAPTER 24

Saul pulled the rollaway bar onto the terrace, poured himself a stiff drink, sat down in a poolside lounger, and pondered his multilayered quandry.

In a sense, Michelle had been right. Galina Rosmanov had indeed changed radically as a result of her experience. But the transformation appeared to have been completely beneficial.

For starters, consider her newfound fluency in English. Or rather her pseudo fluency since, after analyzing the precise nature of her linguistic ability, Saul had deduced that she wasn't actually speaking English but rather projecting her thoughts telepathically directly into his brain. Her words and her facial movements did not coincide because she had not yet become adept enough at the process to transmit without moving her lips.

Then there was her miraculous healing power. That alone could make her the sole subject of a scientific textbook. Or of a New Testament.

And lest he forget her capacity to transport herself without the use of any external paraphernalia. Lest he forget that.

The question was, Why had she been so favorably blessed by her adventure? Granted, short stays inside the bridges tended to have a mildly curative effect. But maintenance men for all the time they spent inside the wires, had never experienced anything even remotely resembling what had happened to Galina.

So apparently there existed some interwire plateau, some point, N hours of continuous interwire habitation, after which the mind transcended its normal limitations and went on to fully develop the complete scope of its unrealized potential. Maintenance men with their repeated entrances and exits simply did not stay inside long enough for the alteration to run its complete spectrum. Only Galina Rosmanov had done that.

But if that were truly the case, then he could only assume this elevated mental state, the ability to go anywhere, speak any language, heal any wound could be attained by *anyone* spending a prolonged period inside the wires. And what would be the end result of that? Would everyone who acquired the power also become as wholesome and as angelic as Galina Rosmanov seemed to have become? Was a magnification of wisdom and judgment an integral part of the process? Would humanity, if given such omnipotence, soar to new heights through mutual co-operation, or plunge into chaos as god battled god for total control of heaven?

And whose responsibility was it to make known the existence of such awesome power? The Bridge Authority? The United States government? The United Nations?

Or Saul himself?

Truly overwhelmed by such philosophical complexities, he switched his focus to a problem of a more practical, although hardly less complex nature. Power and apparent spirituality aside, the fact remained that Galina Rosmanov was still a murderess. If not for her and her poison, Herman Lindstrom might still be alive. But what kind of leg irons could possibly shackle someone able to transport herself through walls?

Was there a limit to her powers? Some substance she could not penetrate? Mythological superheroes always had a weakness, one tiny area of human vulnerability. Superman and Kryptonite. Achilles and his heel. Would there be such a flaw in a real-life superhuman as well?

And suppose a superperson decided to rule the world? Would there be any way for mere mortals to resist?

The clatter of rotor blades jangled Saul back to reality. A helicopter circled the villa once, and floated to a landing on the concrete pad outside his wall.

Saul came around to the front gate just as the helicopter door popped open and Michelle disembarked. She wore a slinky, custom-tailored velour flight suit which, nomenclature notwithstanding, had never been intended to ascend higher into the air than the bar atop the World Trade Center.

Ducking her head out of the way of the rotor blades, she approached the villa's front gate. Her tapping foot kicked up impatient swarms of dust while she waited for Saul to spring the lock.

"Welcome to my humble abode." Saul ushered her in with a steeply overstated bow. "Had I known we were to be graced with the presence of the top enchilada herself, I would have broken out the good silver."

"Instead of your usual matched set of Army surplus mess kits? I'm flattered beyond words." She pushed past him into the villa's front courtyard. "I don't have a lot of time, Saul. So let's skip the preliminaries. Just give me the bridge and let me get on my way."

Saul nodded. "Sure. Gladly. But first, I'd like you to see what that extended stay in the wires did to Galina Rosmanov."

Michelle stopped dead. "Wait a minute. If you want to unload your guilt, see a priest. I told you what she was likely to be. It's your own fault if she came out of there as some kind of monster. You should have left her inside the way I wanted you to."

"Out of sight, out of mind, right? Your office rugs must be getting lumpy from all the dirt you've swept under them over the years."

Michelle made a big point of checking her watch. "I have an important meeting in Rio later on today, and I still have quite a bit of research to do in preparation. So I think I'll pass on the snappy patter, skip the freak show, take the bridge and be gone."

"Galina Rosmanov first, then the bridge. Those are my terms. And they're flatly nonnegotiable."

Michelle jabbed a finger with the force of three evenings a week spent working out at an exclusive European health club. "Saul, you wouldn't be playing it cute with me, would you? We did have a deal you know. You're not planning to renege?"

"You'll get your precious bridge." Saul scooped up her hand and held it hostage between his. "After you see and talk to Galina Rosmanov."

Michelle tried to break away, but failed. So she nodded. "Very well. Have it your way. Trot her out and let's be done with it."

Saul shifted his grip to her elbow, escorted her upstairs and rapped on Galina's door. "Galina. Are you awake? There's someone I'd like you to meet."

"Yes, come in, Saul."

He opened the door. Galina Rosmanov rose from her seat by the window at the far side of the semidarkened room and walked toward them.

"Galina," said Saul, "I'd like you to meet . . ." Saul experienced a momentary rush of dizziness as Galina invaded his mind and deftly extracted the remainder of his statement.

"Yes. Michelle Warren," said Galina. "President of the Bridge Authority." Galina had progressed. She barely moved her lips at all. "So very pleased to meet you."

If Michelle was at all surprised by Galina's apparent normalcy, she hid it quite well. "I'm delighted we were able to get you out safely," she said without even a trace of disconcertment. "Especially so since I must confess to being one of your biggest fans. Your Giselle in Moscow last year. An absolutely brilliant performance." In her sole outward display of bewilderment, Michelle eyed Galina with the thoroughness of someone examining an illusionist's props for hidden doors and false compartments. Michelle sensed that there was something quite odd about Galina, about the way she spoke, but could not quite isolate exactly what it was.

"I'm glad you find pleasure in my work." Galina executed a curtsy, quite gracefully despite the fact she wore one of Saul's caftans, an outfit that gave her the silhouette of a partially disassembled circus tent. She tucked the caftan around her, and sat cross-legged on the bed. "I understand you are Saul's employer."

Michelle studied Galina's lips, trying to decide if the shadows were playing tricks with her, or if she really saw what she thought she did. "What? Oh yes, correct. Saul and I worked quite closely together to get you out. I'm overjoyed that our efforts succeeded."

Galina tilted her head sweetly to one side. "I can appreciate your attempt to misrepresent your role in my rescue, but you should be aware that I am entirely cognizant of the true facts." Her voice bore not the slightest trace of rancor. She might just as well have been discussing the previous day's weather. "I realize full well that if you had gotten your way, I would have been left to dissipate inside the wires."

Michelle gave Saul a scathing look. "You told her," she whispered to him out of the corner of her mouth.

"No, honest. Cross my heart. Not a word."

"Then how did she find out?"

"Search me. Maybe she's psychic," said Saul with a grin, tremendously amused by Michelle's quite atypical state of discomposure.

Michelle interpreted Galina's apparent lack of vindictiveness as a clever tactic designed to throw Michelle off guard. In Michelle's circles, that's how things were done. Never the pistol between the eyes. Always the knife in the back. "I'm terribly sorry for the position I was forced to defend," said Michelle concocting the explanation she felt Galina would be most likely to swallow. "But you must realize that several great scientific minds had me convinced that you would not come out of the wires as a normal individual. I reacted the way I would have wanted someone else to react had that been me in there instead of you. Better to die quickly and painlessly than to spend the rest of your life as a monstrosity."

"Phrased in that manner, a very touching gesture on your part," said Galina with the adorable winsomeness of a girl scout describing the taste of a marshmallow melted between two graham crackers. "Although you did quite conveniently overlook the more self-serving aspects of your actions."

Michelle did not respond. Not because she hadn't a ready answer. No one spontaneously braided lies together better than she. No, she didn't answer because she had finally recognized the extraordinary nature of Galina's manner of speaking. "Saul," Michelle whispered, "when she talks, she doesn't move her lips! What is this, some kind of gag?"

"It's no gag, Michelle," Saul answered. "What's more, it's only the beginning."

Saul addressed Galina directly. "I left the portable wireless bridge downstairs on the dining room table. Would you be good enough to get it, and bring it up here to Michelle?"

"Of course." Galina flashed Saul a conspiratorial grin and vanished. Less than fifteen seconds later she reappeared holding the portable wireless bridge. She handed it to Michelle.

Michelle's mouth flew open, her flawlessly capped teeth protruding like exposed bone in an open wound. An incoherent series of grunts bubbled out of her throat. She was so dumbfounded, she came quite close to fumbling her hard-won bridge onto the floor.

"It has been a real pleasure meeting you, Michelle," said Galina evenly, as though she had just done nothing more than demonstrate an ability to crochet. "Now, if you'll excuse me, I'd like to lie down. I'm still rather exhausted from my experience."

Galina gave Saul a peck on the cheek. Michelle seemed incapable not only of speech but also of movement, so Saul took her by the arm and ushered her into the hallway, no easy task since she kept glancing apprehensively over her shoulder, as if she were being relentlessly pursued by an everwidening crack in the floor of her world.

"Michelle," Galina called after them pleasantly from her doorstep. "Forget about taking me to your lab for study. I won't be poked and prodded like some helpless frog."

Somehow Michelle mustered up a resemblance of righteous indignation. "That's not at all what I . . ."

"I know quite well what you had in mind. You planned to ask me to go in voluntarily and, if I refused, to take me in by force."

Michelle started to argue, but Galina cut her off. "Please don't try to deny it. Just accept the fact that I won't go. And there is no way to force me to do anything I don't want to do. Absolutely no way at all."

Smiling serenely, she closed the door in Michelle's expertly painted face.

CHAPTER 25

Michelle scooped a copy of *Sports Illustrated* off the coffee table and fanned herself with it like some Victorian dowager trying to stave off a swoon. The portable wireless bridge sat neglected on the sofa beside her. "If I hadn't witnessed that with my own eyes!" she said. She looked toward Galina's room, and then sideways at the bridge. With great flourish she rolled her magazine into a tube and thumped it once against her palm to gauge its heft. "Despite the old 'seeing is believing' saw, I can't quite shake the feeling that this entire transaction is nothing but an elaborate hoax aimed at separating me from the bridge."

Saul poured himself a drink. "That's my Michelle. Always suspecting rusted tin under every silver lining." With his glass he gave her a salute to consistency. "On my honor, what little there is of it, what you saw was no fake. Galina Rosmanov can read minds, she can transport herself without the use of a bridge, and something else you didn't see, she can heal other people's injuries."

"Incredible." Michelle tapped her impromptu weapon against her pursed lips like a priest kissing his rosary prior to wrestling a devil. "Do you have any idea what that kind of power portends? Envision bank robbers flitting in and out of vaults. Kidnappers whisking their hapless victims off to God-only-knows where. No way whatsoever for anyone to maintain privacy, either physical or mental. And just suppose it turns out there's no limit to how far someone could travel that way. Why, we could wind up with nobody left on earth."

Saul couldn't suppress a grin. "And what a dent that would put in your next year's profit-and-loss statement."

She ignored his jibe, stood, and walked to the staircase. When she moved, the multiple strands of gold loops encircling her neck clacked together like the dried-bone necklace into which a cannibal chief would tuck his napkin. "We have to act swiftly on this one, before it gets away from us." She placed one foot on the bottom step, apparently ready, if necessary, to race up the stairs and throw her body across the door to prevent Galina's emergence into the course of human affairs. "First we must institute immediate safeguards to prevent this from ever happening again, either on purpose or accidentally. From now on, whenever someone disappears inside the wires they stay there. Permanently. No more Saul Lukas riding in on a white charger to snatch them from the brink of eternity. From now on, it's good-by, Charlie."

Saul grabbed her by the shoulder and pulled her around to face him. To his surprise it was rather like revolving an oak pole imbedded in concrete. "You're taking far too one-sided a view of this. Even if everyone in the world had Galina's power, I don't think the end result would be anywhere near as gloomy as you suppose. You saw that girl. She's only one step removed from sainthood. She's as pure and as compassionate as can be. You worry about thieves? Murderers? Kidnappers? Peeping Toms? I don't think Galina has it in her, and I suspect the same would be true for anyone else undergoing what she did."

"And if you're wrong? What then? Suppose she's not really the Miss Priss she seems to be. Suppose she's learned to mask her true personality completely enough to fool us. Don't forget, you can't evaluate her by human standards anymore. She's as alien to us as we are to cockroaches."

Saul turned his back on her and walked away. "I don't like the direction this conversation is taking. I don't like it one bit. I've known you too long, sweetheart. I can tell where you're headed."

Michelle rushed around and stood in front of him so he could see closeup the depth of her conviction. "There's no alternative, Saul. We must destroy her. I don't like it anymore than you do, but it has to be done. How long do you think it will take her to figure out that she can have anything in this world she wants? Anything. Money, power, adoration."

"And that's a privilege we have to reserve for our current key influentials, present company definitely included."

"That's not it at all. This girl is a threat. If she had come from Mars in a spaceship loaded with laser cannons you wouldn't hesitate a moment to blast her out of existence. But because she's petite and graceful with pretty blue eyes . . ."

"Green. Her eyes are green. And they are quite pretty."

". . . You'll shield her, and protect her, and give her the opportunity to consolidate her power, to grow so strong we can never successfully challenge her, ever again. Don't you see? We must act immediately. Now, while we still have a chance."

Saul sat with both hands pressed to the seat beside him like a bird preparing to spring skyward to escape the jaws of a prowling jackal. "You just can't help but smell dragon smoke in the darkness, can you? But you've overlooked one very real possibility. Instead of being the neighborhood bogeywoman, Galina Rosmanov could just be the savior of humanity, instead. I don't know about you, but I sure don't want history books to remember me as the second man in history to nail a messiah to a cross."

"My God, Saul, you're not talking about a savior. You're talking about the girl that killed your best friend." A bit clumsily, as if she couldn't quite figure out which digits went where, Michelle curled her manicured and lotioned fingers into a fist. "I'm going to do it, Saul, and you can't stop me. If need be I'll mobilize an army with enough firepower to level this villa and everyone in it."

"Great idea. While you parade around outside playing Alexander the Great, Galina transports herself to Buenos Aires or Port-au-Prince, or any of a thousand other places. Remember, Galina reads minds. There's no way to surprise that girl. She'll know your plans almost the instant you do."

"I'll find a way, Saul. She can't be invincible. She must have a flaw. I'll find it and turn it against her."

"Best of luck, sweetheart, but I think you're chasing the wind. Galina Rosmanov is here to stay. And I personally don't think that's such a bad prospect. I feel the world will wind up being a better place because of her presence."

"And I think you're dead wrong."

"Your perogative, after all it is a free country."

"But maybe not for long."

Suddenly they heard a helicopter chugging in overhead. Not the small, two-seater variety Michelle had arrived in, but the bigger type used by construction companies to transport heavy materials to the tops of tall buildings.

"Who do you suppose that could be?" Saul wondered aloud as he watched it overfly the villa. He saw perhaps as many as fifteen people bunched together at the helicopter's open door. "The press," he said. "It must be the press. Here to interview Galina."

"We can't let that happen, Saul." From out of her shoulder bag Michelle pulled a pistol, so small it could have been a toy. "We can't let the outside world discover what she's like."

Saul nearly burst out laughing when Michelle shifted her tiny weapon into a two-handed grip. "Wait," he said. "I'll hunt up my bean shooter, we'll go out on the lawn, and stage a showdown for the evening news."

Michelle had her back to the window. Looking over her shoulder, Saul watched the helicopter descend. Less than fifteen seconds later a number of grappling hooks sailed across the wall. Granted reporters tended to be overzealous, but . . . Then he saw the first of the climbers drop over into the courtyard. No reporter that one, not unless reporters had taken to gathering news with the aid of Uzi submachine guns. "Michelle," he said, "those guys aren't reporters. They're commandos of some kind."

Michelle smiled wryly. "Somehow I expected better of you, Saul. They don't even use that old 'look behind you' dodge in the movies anymore."

Machine-gun fire echoed across the courtyard as one of the commandos fired a disabling burst into the wheels of the jeep Saul kept in the driveway.

When Michelle turned her head toward the window, Saul plucked the gun out of her hands. She didn't even appear to notice it missing. "My God," she said as she watched the commandos storm the villa. "Who are they?"

"Beats me. Russians maybe. Or Israelis." Saul pointed to the portable wireless bridge. "We've got a pretty desirable piece of merchandise in here with us. I suspect there are any number of groups who would love to relieve us of it." He pushed her toward the door. "Quick. Into the den. I'll bridge you and the device out in my private transportal."

Saul could tell when they reached the den, though, that there would be no escape by transportal today. The system, which even on standby sparkled with more lights than a Christmas tree, was completely dark. Every function monitor told him the same story. Off the air. Incredible. Such a thing wasn't supposed to be possible. These private units, because of the high-priority passengers they carried, were the most secure in the network. Every circuit triply shielded. A backup for every safety device. Linking cables encased in three feet of solid concrete to foil saboteurs. Oh, someone's head would roll for this. Assuming, of course, there was anyone alive afterward to tell the tale.

Then it suddenly dawned on him that there was still a slender hope. There was someone in the villa who could still easily go for help. "Galina," he shouted from the bottom of the staircase. "Galina, get . . ." Something hard hit him in the small of the back. He crumpled to the floor and rolled over to see Mary Hemke standing above him, a malicious leer on her face. Like Michelle, Mary Hemke too wore a flight suit. But hers was discolored by oil spots. And a maroon stain, which Saul suspected was dried blood, framed a small hole in the upper arm. A long way from the top of the World Trade Center, this garment.

"I guess this means I don't get my ten million dollar finder's fee," said Saul.

"A logical assumption," said Mary Hemke. She pointed her machine gun at his head.

Saul abandoned all thoughts of resistance. The odds against success were far too high. "You'll find the bridge in the den on the floor in front of the transportal," he said. "By the way, how did you shut that thing down?"

"Magic," Mary said using her machine gun to motion one of her men into the den. The man emerged seconds later carrying the portable wireless bridge under one arm, Michelle under the other.

"No," shouted Michelle. "No, you can't have it. You don't understand. It can't be put into use."

"If she says another word," Mary told one of the two commandos in the room, "shoot her." So much for a willingness to negotiate.

Mary took the portable wireless bridge from her soldier and hefted it. "So this is the little devil." She stroked it with her palm. "O.K." she told her comrades. "Let's move." Her men darted out the front door. Keeping Saul and Michelle covered, Mary backed out after them. She had one foot planted on the top step when Galina's door opened, and Galina stepped out onto the second-floor landing. "Saul," she called down. "Is something wrong?"

"Hold it a minute," said Mary to her men. She re-entered the villa. "That's Galina Rosmanov, isn't it?" she asked no one in particular. "Get down here, honey." She motioned toward Galina with her gun.

Slowly, Galina descended the stairs.

"Come on, shake it, lady." Mary pointed impatiently toward the front door with her gun. "You're going with us."

"What could you possibly want with her?" asked Saul.

"Seed money to help us get our bridge production started. I have a hunch the Russians will pay big to get back a celebrity cupcake like this. Come on, honey." She prodded Galina with her weapon. "Move."

"I don't want to go with you," said Galina firmly.

"You think you've got a choice?" said Mary. She slammed her hand in the small of Galina's back propelling her out the door.

"Pleasure doing business with you," Mary said to Michelle and Saul.

Abruptly, without warning, Mary clutched at her throat, first with one hand, then, dropping her weapon, with two. Her face reddening, she sank, gasping, to her knees. Saul ran to her. Through the open doorway he saw that all of her men were doing the same, thrashing on the ground, clutching at their throats and gasping for air.

Galina stood on the front steps, her eyes closed and her lips pressed tightly together like a child in the grip of a nightmare.

"That's enough," Saul shouted at Galina. "Ease off." He put his hand to Mary Hemke's pulse. It fluttered several times, and then stopped. Saul dropped the woman's lifeless wrist and stood. "My God," he said to Michelle. "She's dead."

"They were going to hurt me," said Galina brushing past him as she came back inside. "I read it in their minds. They frightened me, made me lose control." Tears streamed down her face. "I didn't want to hurt them. I don't want to hurt anyone, ever again." She turned, darted up the stairs and shut herself into her room.

"What do you think of your harmless little Barbie doll now?" asked Michelle looking out at the bodies littering the front courtyard.

"You heard her. It was an accident."

"Was it, now? Was it really?" Michelle picked up the portable wireless bridge and examined it closely for damage.

CHAPTER 26

Michelle reacted with customary dispatch.

Within an hour, a gang of men descended on Saul's villa by helicopter. They wore no uniforms, displayed no insignia. A thorough shakedown wouldn't have turned up so much as a library card among them. They spoke to each other in a polyglot mixture of German, French, and English, mercenaries' tongues, prime languages of the men who go to war the way other men go to the office.

Without wasted motion, acting as though they had performed this same function countless times before, the men collected the fallen bodies—there turned out to be eighteen total—and stuffed them into canvas bodybags, which they stacked neatly inside their helicopter. When finished, they took off in the direction of the collector station the Bridge Authority maintained fifteen kilometers away in Oaxa.

Michelle left with them, taking the portable wireless bridge along.

A short while later, Saul heard a local radio announcer report that eighteen members of One World United, including infamous urban guerrilla Mary Hemke, had perished in a helicopter crash half the world away, on the outskirts of Havana. The report made no mention whatsoever of the Bridge Authority, Galina Rosmanov, or portable wireless bridges.

Saul flicked off the radio and headed for the kitchen, threading his way through the web of cabling and instruments being used by the Bridge Authority technicians repairing his private transportal. Mary Hemke's group had penetrated the concrete shielding and severed both the main and the backup transmittal wires with a laser cannon stolen several months earlier from a National Guard

Armory in Duluth. A permanent fix would require several days. In the meantime, the technicians had strung in a temporary, unsecured wire through normal underground conduit. They had already activated it and were in the process of calibrating it. When they finished, a maintenance man would give the hookup one final internal checkout, and Saul's transportal would again be operational. The entire process would take anywhere from twelve to twenty hours, depending on how swiftly the calibration went. As a tideover, the Bridge Authority had placed several helicopters at Saul's disposal. If he wanted to bridge out, one of the helicopters would ferry him to the Oaxa collector station. From there he could catch a ride to anywhere in the world.

Though, after the frantic travel of the past few days, for the present he was more than content to remain in one place for a while. He rummaged through the refrigerator, found the necessary ingredients for a ham on rye, and built them into a sandwich that he carried upstairs.

He knocked on Galina's door. "Come in, Saul," she said.

He found her sitting on the floor amid a huge ring of Russian language true romance magazines one of the technicians had carted in for her. "I thought you might like something to eat," he said.

"That's very kind of you," she answered, "but I have no appetite." She flipped through story after story in futile search for a happy ending.

"Do you want to talk about what happened?" Saul asked.

Galina nodded, an action that sent twin ribbons of tears floating across her cheeks. "I couldn't help myself. I didn't realize my power could be so destructive. Until that awful moment, I regarded it exclusively in the positive sense, as something to be used for the good of mankind. I swear to you, Saul, I would rather die than to ever again be responsible for another such dreadfully inhumane action."

Saul took out his handkerchief and dried her tears. "I believe you. But I'm afraid there are others who don't."

"Michelle Warren," she said. "Yes, I know. I read it in her thoughts." With her finger Galina traced a line from one of her ears to the other. It was the same line a noose would follow if tightened around her neck. "She wants me dead. She is even this instant busily conferring with her legal staff to see if there exists ample evidence to have me executed for Herman Lindstrom's murder."

Saul studied her face with the piercing scrutiny of a jeweler examining a diamond for flaws. "You don't plan to do anything rash, anything aggressive? Get her before she gets you?"

Galina shook her head evoking the free-spirited determination of a range mare resolved never to be broken to saddle and bit. "Certainly not! I told you, I find that part of me disgusting. I will never let it surface again. No, I will counter her in a much more inventive manner. I will monitor her thoughts, as I am doing even now, and, through foreknowledge, negate whatever ploys she initiates against me. It will consume a major portion of my concentration, but, at least for the immediate future, I see no alternative. She's a very strong-willed woman, but I detect a certain practicality in her, too. When she finally realizes that I have no desire to destroy either her or her empire, she'll go on about her business and leave me alone."

"And when that time comes, what will you do?"

"I don't know." She anchored her hand to his. "I thought you might help me decide. I want to put my talents to work in the best possible way, but I'm not quite sure how to go about it." She poked her fingers upward, as if the solution to her dilemma had just flown by at shoulder level and she had only to spear it out of the air. "Perhaps I should emulate the characters in so many of your American comic books. Affect a secret identity. Use my ballet dancing as a cover to battle crime and injustice throughout the world." Squaring off her hands, she formed a frame around her face. "How do you think I would look in a black mask and cape?"

Saul shook his head and laughed. "Like one of the featured players in the movies I used to smuggle into the States from Tijuana."

She poked Saul's handkerchief into the corners of her eyes to forestall another burst of tears. "Please, don't tease. I'm quite serious about this. I really do find it quite a problem, deciding how to best apply my talents."

Saul knelt down beside her and took her into his arms. She seemed custom-made for the position. "Galina, have patience. This whole thing is just too new for you to swallow in one gulp. I have a hunch that as time goes by things will fall into line, and your best course of action will become quite clear. You'll do what's right. I have absolutely no doubt."

She threw her arms around his neck and kissed him. "I don't know what I'd do without you. You should despise me for what I did to your best friend. But instead you give me tender, gentle support and the self-confidence I need to survive."

Because, as far as he was concerned, the Galina he held in his arms had no more relationship to the Galina who had gone into the wires than a caterpillar had to a butterfly.

"I feel exactly the same way," she said reading his thoughts. "I am a totally different person, a better person. But only you believe that."

He stared deep into her eyes and saw there the future of the world. "In time, everyone else will believe it, too. Starting with Michelle."

She cuddled herself into the hollows of his body like a forest animal burrowing in against the icy blasts of winter. "With all my heart and soul, I do so hope you're right."

CHAPTER 27

Saul scuttled up the marble staircase and into the Moscow Palace of Fine Arts with the enthusiasm of a man ascending to the gallows. He had agreed to subject himself to the twin agonies of classical music and a rented tuxedo only because this marked Galina's first public performance since her disappearance, and she had begged him to be present.

In the foyer he found the gold bust of Lenin where, by prearrangement, he was to meet Rosie. He leaned against Lenin's shoulder for support while he took in the passing parade of blow-styled hair, manicured fingernails, tailored dresses, and floor-length furs. A department-store window come almost to life.

One of the more stunning of the animated mannikins broke away from the others and approached him. It was Michelle. She wore a green dress, which clung to her like the thin film on the surface of day-old lime Jello. Looking at her, Saul remembered their sky-rocket trip to the stars. Then she spoke and brought him crashing back to earth.

"Excuse me, sir," she said, "but I'm afraid you've accidentally wandered into the ballet. The ladies' nude wrestling matches are two blocks down."

Saul hooked his thumbs into his suspenders and pulled them into the shape of a bum with delusions of grandeur. "Nope, no accident at all. Part of my new image. From here on I'm one hundred per cent couth." He reached for where his cigarettes usually were, but encountered only a handful of lace. Since tuxedos no longer bore pockets, he had been informed by the rental agency that he would have to chose between going the entire evening without a smoke or carrying an evening bag. That's when he decided to invite Rosie, and her biggest purse, to attend the ballet with him. "Somehow I didn't expect to see you here," he told Michelle.

She chucked him coquettishly under the chin with her feather boa. "Why, sweetie, I wouldn't have missed it for the world. After all, how often does one get to see a living legend resurrected from the dead." She wrapped her boa around one arm and her male secretary around the other.

"I've got to say," Saul admitted rather grudgingly, "that you've treated Galina with a lot more restraint than I ever expected." During the four months Galina had been living with Saul at his villa, Michelle had not intruded in the slightest. From Michelle's thoughts, Galina divined that Michelle had adopted a wait-and-see attitude. So long as Galina behaved herself, Michelle would let her alone. And that is exactly what Galina had done. Behaved herself.

Although certain tangential aspects of Galina's personality were impossible to conceal—her noticeably more pronounced effort to accommodate the feelings of others, her outward composure, her inner serenity—for the most part she had kept her powers a total secret.

Her second month out of the wires she had returned to the Kirov.

Saul had gone with her to the rehearsal hall a few times to watch her prepare for her comeback. From the comments of her fellow dancers, Saul gathered that her dancing had changed as radically as her personality.

She had originally risen to stardom on the strength of a supreme technical virtuosity. Her flair for creative interpretation had been rated, at best, average. But now that had changed. She had retained her technical artistry, but had bolstered it with a deeper spirit, imbuing each movement with an almost luminous intensity she had never evidenced before.

"So, how are you two love birds getting along?" asked Michelle.

"We struggle through," Saul answered. "And while we're on the subject of emotional involvements, how's work coming on the portable bridge?"

Michelle glanced warily up at Lenin's ear. "Quite well, actually. After we worked out the mechanics of it, we sold it to the military. We began limited production a few days ago. I'm projecting two units a week to start, escalating to ten a week after six months. Naturally, we're keeping internal workings proprietary. Every unit will be sealed and rigged with a self-destruct mechanism to prevent anyone from opening it and examining its innards. In sum, I'd say everything worked out quite well."

"I'll tell that to Herman Lindstrom next time I bump into him."

Michelle flashed him a smile as hollow as the inside of a cannon barrel. And nearly as lethal. "I didn't want to get into that, lover, but since you brought it up, be aware that as far as Herman Lindstrom goes, I've got your sweet young girlfriend cold. I've got a safe full of murder-one evidence against her. So you tell her for me that she either toes the line or takes a one-way trip to sizzle city."

Saul looped an arm around her shoulder and gave her a lecherous squeeze. "I just love it when you talk tough," he said in a lisping falsetto.

Michelle untangled herself from him and fluffed up her boa's feathers. Not a one dared to come out in her hand. "I'm serious, Saul. She crosses me, she's dead." She wrapped her boa around her like a mantle of justice. "Enjoy the show," she said. "And, in the interest of cultural propriety, I'll expect you to restrain your normal impulse to yell 'Take it off' the first time a girl appears on stage."

Dragging her secretary along beside her, she entered the auditorium.

Rosie pulled in just as Saul was about to begin stopping passers-by at random in quest of a smoke. She opened her purse, handed him a pack and a lighter.

"You just missed Michelle," he said stroking the lighter to life.

"That ruins my entire evening," she said, feigning disappointment. "Maybe I can catch her after the show when she goes to the check room to pick up her broom."

They stood there, face to face, in silence, like two close siblings caught on opposite sides of a civil war. They hadn't seen each other much lately, not since Galina moved into Saul's life. Rosie made her uncomfortable, she said, and until she could overcome that feeling, she would much appreciate it if Saul didn't bring Rosie around. Thus she had accomplished in a few sentences the disassociation that Michelle had been trying to bring about for years.

"And how's Galina doing?" said Rosie to break the silence.

"Great. No problems. We've been doing some tests, the two of us, to see if we can track the limits of her power. Thus far we've found that her transmission range extends to about a thousand kilometers, although she can go farther if she travels in stages since her recovery time after a jump is practically nil. She can transport up to three kilos along with her, but only if it's inert matter. She can't dematerialize living things."

"What about her healing powers?"

"Apparently restricted to transference-related damage. She can't heal so much as a razor nick otherwise."

"And her telepathy?"

"That's a strange one. There's no distance limitation on her ability to read minds, but there is an inverse recovery rate involved. She can read a mind on the other side of the world, but only for an hour or so, and the ability then disappears for nearly half a day afterward."

"Can she penetrate any mind at will?"

"No, she can be blocked out. I can do it, my houseboy can do it, but it takes a while to learn the technique and requires quite a bit of mental discipline."

"Worth it, though, if you value your privacy."

"True." He snuffed out his cigarette, took Rosie by the arm, and escorted her toward the door. When they were in their seats, he looked up from his program and said, almost as an afterthought, "You know, Michelle and I disagree radically concerning Galina. She thinks Galina is the worst disaster to hit the world since the black plague. I think Galina's the greatest thing since sliced bread. What's your opinion?"

Rosie shook her head like a naval wife scanning the horizon for sight of a lost ship. "I honestly don't know. She doesn't give off any vibrations, positive or negative. In the few times I've been with her long enough to probe her, I got nothing, like she didn't even exist. It's never happened to me before. I've always been able to pick up something. She's either so different that I can't fathom her, or she's consciously freezing me out."

"Why would she do that?" asked Saul.

"Only one reason I can think of." She finally put into words what she had wanted to tell him from the start. "Perhaps she's got something to hide."

The lights dimmed and the curtain went up.

The company was performing *The Censor,* a ballet especially choreographed for a strong, graceful ballerina, and Galina danced the role to perfection. Her partner seemed almost superfluous. She appeared quite able to float through the air without him.

At the final curtain the applause piled up on stage as deeply as the bouquets of flowers.

After almost half an hour, when the ovation finally subsided, Saul went backstage where he found Galina besieged by reporters and translators in about equal proportions.

"Elaine's?" she asked Saul telepathically while she waited for one of the interpreters to translate a question that she had, of course, already plucked from the mind of the reporter who had asked it.

Saul would have preferred one of the quiet, workingmen's bars he frequented on New York's Lower East Side, but this was her night, and if she wanted to spend it consorting with snobs, so be it. "Sure, Elaine's," he said under his breath. He realized he did not have to vocalize his words for her to pick them up, but, despite a great deal of practice, he was still unable to suppress sound when he addressed her.

"You leave now," she said mentally. "I'll meet you there in an hour." While Saul would ride wire to New York, Galina would travel direct.

Saul hopped a cab to the Moscow terminal, bridged to New York, and from recovery, caught a cab to Elaine's. Galina was already there waiting for him when he arrived.

"Did you enjoy the performance?" she asked him.

"Sensational." He signaled to the waiter and ordered them drinks. For her an orange juice straight. Since her emergence from the wires, she had lost her desire for both alcohol and tobacco. Thus far, thank God, it hadn't rubbed off on him. For himself he ordered a double Bourbon over ice and a Cuban cigar.

He had barely touched either when he saw Felice Pierenska enter the restaurant. Galina's triumphant return had relegated Felice once again to a supporting role in the Kirov's corps de ballet. When she saw Galina, she headed straight for their table, waving her hand and screeching drunkenly in Russian. Even though he didn't speak a word of the language, Saul had no trouble deciphering her message. She obviously disliked her demotion and deeply resented Galina for having brought it about.

Galina attempted to calm her down, but the girl refused to be placated. In fact, she probably would have been more than willing to decide which one danced first string by going to best two out of three falls right there on Elaine's floor. She unleashed another verbal outburst, reached down, grabbed Galina's glass, and flung the contents into Galina's face.

Saul's brain nearly exploded under the impact of Galina's rage. For a horrible instant he feared she would lose control and throttle her youthful adversary the same way she had Mary Hemke and her commandos. But apparently Galina had meant what she said about suppressing the malevolent aspect of her personality. Her anger subsided almost as rapidly as it had built. She dried her face as best she could with her napkin, and stood. Head high, holding Saul's hand firmly for support, she brushed past Felice and walked out the door. A magnificent lady every step of the way.

The next morning Saul regarded the incident with Felice as nothing more than an ugly footnote to a splendid accomplishment. At least he did until he read his morning paper.

The front page carried two stories side by side.

One heralded Galina's return. The other detailed how Felice Pierenska, after creating a public disturbance in an unnamed fashionable New York night spot, had gone home to Madrid where she had thrown herself off the balcony of her twenty-sixth floor apartment.

Despite the fact that those living on either side of her reported hearing the sounds of a loud argument just prior to her jump, neighbors who had broken into her apartment only moments later had found the place empty. According to the story, police would continue to investigate, but, in the absence of any credible evidence of foul play, would almost certainly wind up dismissing the incident as a suicide.

Saul reread the story carefully, paying close attention to the time factors involved. The paper stated Felice had gone out the window at 6 A.M. Figuring in the seven-hour time differential, that would have made it 11 P.M. at Saul's villa.

Almost precisely the time he had been awakened last night by Galina returning to bed.

She had gone downstairs, she said, for a glass of water. Of course, in the time it took for a normal person to travel from Saul's bedroom to his kitchen sink and back, Galina Rosmanov could easily have taken a round trip to an apartment in Madrid.

He carried the paper upstairs and handed it to Galina. "Know anything about this?" he asked.

Galina took the paper from him and read the story through. "The poor girl," she said when she had finished. "Such potential. Wasted." She set the paper aside, took Saul's hand and pressed it to her lips with a great deal of tenderness, as though it was the most important thing she would do that day. "Of course I know nothing about it. Why do you ask?" She pulled him down beside her and stroked his temple. "You keep yourself closed off from me so much lately. I begin to suspect you don't trust me." Her eyes widened into the shape of the danger signs on a winding mountain road. "You think I had something to do with her death. That's what you believe, isn't it? You think that because she made a fool of me, I sneaked away in the middle of the night and shoved her off her balcony."

"Did you?"

"Of course not." She twitched like a frightened, helpless rabbit about to be clubbed to death by a stone-age barbarian. "You know yourself that I've grown incapable of hostility."

"No, you've repressed it. There is a difference."

"In semantic terms only. As far as I'm concerned, I've grown incapable of it. If you don't believe me, if you think I'm lying to you, well, perhaps it's time we re-evaluated our relationship." She rolled over and put her back to him.

He stroked her shoulder and tendered the unconditional surrender which so often ends a battle of love. "I'm sorry, pumpkin," he said. "Please forgive me for doubting you. It's just that sometimes my natural distrust overshadows my rationality."

She rolled over and embraced him. "Oh, Saul. You can be so silly. Nevertheless, I do love you so much."

He stood up. "Tell you what. How about if for a peace offering I bridge over to Paris and have that chef you like so well at Maxim's whip us up a picnic basket for later on today. Maybe we could take a hike through Yosemite or someplace. Would you like that?"

She squeezed his hand. "It would be delightful."

He went downstairs to his private transportal. "I'll be out for a few hours," he told his houseboy. "Do me a favor, would you? Phone up Maxim's in Paris and have them bridge out a picnic lunch for two. And tell them none of that frou-frou stuff, O.K.? Something I can get my teeth into. Have them stick in a half-dozen of those good cigars they keep around for after dinner, plus a six-pack of beer."

Saul set the transportal's destination controls. "And block it out of your mind, would you? I don't want Galina to find out that you got the stuff instead of me."

Saul pressed the transmit button. He awoke an hour later in Madrid.

CHAPTER 28

Roberto Fernandez, captain of the Madrid police force, slipped a dusty bottle of Spanish brandy out of his bottom desk drawer. The two of them, he and the bottle, had a great deal in common. They were both the same age, both the same mellow brown color, and they could both lull people into saying things they'd deeply regret the next morning.

Fernandez cracked the bottom half of his face open into the toothy gash he considered a smile. An ugly white scar, souvenir of a nighttime encounter with a section of lead pipe, wormed the length of his right jaw. The area to the rear of the scar, under his right ear, had been rebuilt by a plastic surgeon. Further out, toward the chin, the bone caved sharply inward where the surgeon had either run out of plastic or run out of hope. Fernandez's uniform looked freshly washed, although the way its wrinkles contoured to his body suggested that he had been standing inside it at the time. On the corner of his desk, where other men displayed pictures of their wives and children, he kept his gun.

"I hear through the grapevine that you been laid off." Fernandez pushed the bottle across to Saul's side of the desk. "From now on, so I hear, anybody who gets caught in the wires stays there. No more Saul Lukas to the rescue. That true?" His words slurred out in fuzzy, brandy-wrapped bundles. Saul could not recall ever having seen him completely sober. But then neither had he ever seen him completely drunk.

"True enough." Saul tipped some of the brandy into a glass so grimy he was hard pressed to gauge the level of his slug. "I'm apparently unemployed."

"No problem. You come here for a job, my friend, you got it." Fernandez repossessed the brandy, wiped the mouth with his palm, and took a healthy belt straight from the bottle. "Of course there are formalities. You have to be investigated for anti-Communist sympathies clear back to when your uncles had tails. You have to take a loyalty oath to Mother Russia. You have to give up your fancy villa and come live in state-owned housing in Madrid. You have to turn all your personal property over to the government. You have to attend political orientation classes five nights a week. You have to take orders from a party commissar who tells you you've got the wrong man if you arrest anybody except for a priest, a capitalist, a political dissident, or a Jew." He tilted the bottle skyward again. "I think in the final analysis, you're better off collecting welfare."

Saul raised his glass. "Thanks for the advice. I hearby formally withdraw my application."

"Think nothing of it." Fernandez wiped his mouth on the corner of the Russian flag beside his desk. "What really brings you to Madrid?"

Saul finished his brandy and waved off Fernandez's attempt to pour him more. "I'm checking out a suicide. A young ballerina. Felice Pierenska. Happened yesterday morning around six. She took a dive out of her apartment window."

"Oh yes, that one." Fernandez pulled out and lit something that smelled like it had last been used to secure an anchor to a ship. "A cut-and-dried case. A high-strung girl, despondent about having been relegated to a lesser position with her dance company, she had one too many drinks, decided she couldn't take it any more, so she jumped. Typical pattern."

"Any note?"

Fernandez tapped a chunk of dead ash off the end of his cigar and stared introspectively at the glowing tip beneath. "No."

They both knew that suicides rarely went without a note. Still, it did happen, and, by itself, proved nothing.

"What about the voices the neighbors heard? Just before she jumped? Anything on that?"

Fernandez put his feet on his desk beside his gun and his bottle. "That's a strange one. The guy next door broke into her place not eight seconds after he heard her scream. She lived near the dead end of a long corridor, so if anybody had just left her place, he would have seen them. But he saw nobody. And there was nobody inside her place, either. It's only two and a half rooms with bath, and he checked it out good. The place was empty. No doubt about it. But the neighbors still swear they heard someone in there with her."

"A man, a woman, which?"

"A woman. She spoke Russian. The neighbors spoke only Spanish, so they couldn't tell me what the two of them said."

"You checked the television and radio listings for that time period, I suppose."

"First thing. Nothing on with that kind of dialogue."

"Did you autopsy her?"

"Of course." He pointed toward a row of red-bound books gathering dust on a table behind him. "There are some regulations I don't ignore."

"Anything suspicious?"

"Nothing concrete." Fernandez hunched over from the weight of the inconsistencies piled up on his back. "She died from the fall. No question about that. But the medical boys also found evidence of strangulation. Anoxia in the brain. Ruptured blood vessels in the lungs. Although there was nothing external to back it up. No finger marks or bruises on the neck. No damage to the windpipe. Almost as if somebody strangled her by remote control, and she fell off the balcony by accident while trying to catch her breath." He peered into his bottle, but the answer wasn't there. "Although we both know that's impossible. Don't we, Saul?"

"Yeah," said Saul standing to go. "We sure do."

CHAPTER 29

Billowy clouds so incredibly uniform they almost restored Saul's faith in travel brochures drifted over the Swiss meadow Galina had chosen for their picnic. While Saul sat on their blanket drinking a beer, Galina, her graceful body playing peek-a-boo through the two yards of filmy, colored gauze she called a dress, explored a nearby hill.

With one hand hidden behind her, she approached Saul and knelt down beside him. "For you." With great fanfare she produced a bouquet of wild flowers.

"Very nice, thank you." He pulled one of the flowers free and sequentially removed its petals. When there was only one remaining, he held it up for her to see. "According to this, you love me not."

"Just goes to show you can never trust a flower." Galina pulled him to her and gave him a kiss that, set to music, would have easily reached the top forty. But Saul didn't respond, prompting Galina to ask why.

Saul killed his beer and laid the soldier beside its four dead comrades. "I guess I'm just concerned about your future, about your ability to protect yourself should Michelle or anyone else try to harm you."

Her laughter floated off like one of those deceptively tiny mountain streams that gradually grows into a torrent and eventually becomes the sea. "Let me assure you that you have absolutely nothing to fear. I'm not nearly as fragile as you seem to believe, nor am I totally defenseless." She opened the last beer and handed it to him. "Remember when we did those tests to determine my limits? How long ago? Two months perhaps? Well, as it turns out, we were a bit premature. I'm apparently still evolving. If we redid those same tests today, we would find my powers have at least doubled. And that's only my best guess. Some of them may have tripled. I can monitor several minds simultaneously now, and over longer distances. I can travel direct to any point on the globe. And, even more marvelous . . ." At this point Saul had to stop her and ask her to repeat herself because what she was saying excited her so that she had inadvertently lapsed into verbal Russian, and Saul didn't catch a word.

"A few days ago," she said on second run-through, "completely by accident, I discovered I can manipulate people, walk them around like marionettes, make them do almost anything I want them to. Can you believe it?"

"I don't know. I'm not sure I understand exactly what you mean. Could you show me?"

"Of course." She made a seductive motion with her lips. "How about if I have you make love to me?"

Saul pressed his fingertips to her mouth and shook his head. "Too easy. For that I'm a pushover. Make it something else, something I would normally never do of my own free will."

Her voice tumbled down into some shadowy pit and her eyes followed. "I'd rather not experiment on you that way. It would smack too much of the awful things scientists do to rats."

"Please. I insist. I want to see this new talent in action. You have my complete absolution in advance for whatever happens."

She turned both her palms toward the sky like a reluctant ball-player hoping to catch enough last-minute moisture to get the game called on account of rain. "Very well, but remember, you forced me into it."

She shut her eyes.

That's all there was to it. No other outward manifestations whatsoever. She simply shut her eyes, and Saul fell instantly to all fours.

"Speak." She held up her hand. In it Saul saw a bone-shaped dog biscuit.

Saliva gushed out across his lower lip. He barked until his throat turned raw.

Galina moved her hand over his head. "Sit up and beg."

Invisible strings jerked Saul to his hind legs. His arms extended in front of him. His wrists went limp. And he begged. Oh, how he begged. To get that biscuit he would have heeled, fetched, rolled over, played dead, chased a cat up a tree, or torn a postman to shreds.

Galina opened her eyes, and the phenomenon ended as instantaneously as it had begun.

"You see what I mean?" said Galina. "And I barely warmed up. If I set my mind to it, I believe I could literally make anyone do anything. So you needn't worry about my being harmed. I definitely have the means to prevent it."

"So you do." The Goliath of the ant world shoved a bread crumb across Saul's ankle. Saul tried to imagine what it would be like to live ant fashion, existing solely to serve the needs of an insatiable queen. It certainly had its advantages. A simple life-style, a clear-cut goal, plenty of camaraderie. Ants probably loved it.

"And there's something else. I also have another new talent." She reclaimed one of her flowers and picked at its petals. "I now also possess the ability to pass any or all of my powers on to other people."

It took Saul a moment to get over the shock. "I'm flabbergasted. I don't know what to say. Are you going to do it? Are you going to bestow your powers on someone else?"

She plucked off one of her flower's last two petals. "Yes, I am. I'm going to share all of my powers with you." She held up the flower, rotating it so its single petal stood up straight between them. "Because I love you so very much."

Saul took the flower from her and spun it between his fingers. The last petal tore loose and floated away on the air. "I seem to recall someone telling me not too very long ago that I should never trust a flower."

Galina pointed the same finger young cowboys use to shoot imaginary Indians. "We're no longer talking in hypotheses and parables. We're discussing reality. I'm prepared to give you powers other men have only dreamed about, to shape you in my own image, to make you the second member of the new human race. It would defy all rationality for you to say no."

"I must admit it does have its appeal." He zipped his windbreaker up around the lump in his throat. "Still, you have to remember that deep down I'm just a simple guy. It's a pretty radical change you're proposing here. I'd like to give it some thought."

"Of course." She settled back and relaxed like someone who had wagered a great deal of money on the only horse in the race. The question was not would she win, but how soon before her horse crossed the finish line so she could cash in her tickets. "Take as long as you need. I'll transform you whenever you're ready."

He lay awake the better part of the night considering her offer. When he had finally decided, he got out of bed, dressed, entered his private transportal, and went to see Michelle.

CHAPTER 30

Despite the late hour, Michelle looked stunning, like something modeled from out of the same pixie dust and water used to concoct the plaster reality that advertising agencies pass off as real life. Perfectly ordered hair, flawless makeup, exactly the proper touch of perfume, voguish dressing gown. A deodorant commercial personified, right down to the dry armpits.

"Let me guess," she said brightly when she answered his knock on the door connecting her beach-front mansion to the room housing her private transportal. "You couldn't sleep so you popped by to see if I would go soft-hearted on the property settlement and give you back your teddy bear."

Saul jammed his hands and his pride into the back pockets of his jeans. "Look, I'm not very proficient at this apology stuff, so do me a favor and lighten up on the wisecracks."

"Apology? For what?"

He nodded his head toward the room behind her. "Maybe we could talk about it inside."

"Sure," said Michelle. "Of course. Be with you in a minute." She closed the door.

He heard a pair of mumbled voices, one of them distinctly male. An inside door slammed shut, Michelle returned, and told Saul to come inside.

Saul followed her to the bar where she produced a bottle of cheap Bourbon. "Looks familiar," he said.

"It should. It's one of your leftover personal effects."

"Saving it as a memento?"

"Hardly. I put it out with the trash every week, but the sanitation department keeps rejecting it as below minimum standards for the neighborhood."

"Thank God for discriminating garbage men," said Saul toasting the cast-iron stomachs of the world.

While he poured himself a refill, Michelle blended four liqueurs, a dash of bitters, several egg whites, a mound of sugar, and some crushed ice into a concoction with a lot more froth than wallop. "I assume this late-night visitation has something to do with Galina."

Saul sat down on the sofa and, ignoring Michelle's pronounced wince, propped his feet on a coffee table whose sculpted wooden legs duplicated the wispy underpinnings of an elderly canary. "Let me start off by emphasizing that I don't have a single shred of hard backup for anything I'm about to tell you. I'm basing my conclusions exclusively on circumstantial evidence. But there's enough of that to cause me a great deal of concern." Thus, he unfolded his story, the incident at Elaine's, the mysterious circumstances surrounding Felice Pierenska's suicide, Galina's newest talent, and finally Galina's offer to invest him with her powers.

"I judge from your sternly disapproving air," Michelle said when he had finished, "that you're going to pass up superman status in favor of plodding along same as always with us ordinary folks."

"You got it. I've gradually come to doubt whether anyone with that kind of power, even a saint, could resist for very long the temptation to forcibly inflict his will, and his beliefs, upon everybody else. Supermen operate fine in comic books. In real life their capes tend to get tangled up in their selfish human egos. Sure Galina can perform miracles. But underneath that, I guess her basic nature hasn't changed in the slightest. She was a murderess before; she's a murderess after. The only difference is that now she's better at concealing it."

"Don't act so betrayed," said Michelle topping off his glass. "You're certainly not the first guy to be jolted awake right in the middle of a beautiful dream." She settled into an easy chair and folded her hands across her chest like a victorious general confronting the opposition's only surviving soldier. "What we've got to do now is decide how to handle her." She swung her index finger in any easy semicircle like someone dialing a very familiar number. "Any suggestions?"

Saul put a cigarette in his mouth and watched it go up in

smoke right along with his scruples. "I figured we'd do it your way."

She cocked her head to emphasize her bewilderment. "I beg your pardon? Do it my way? I don't understand."

"Come off it. You know perfectly well what I mean."

"I'm afraid I don't. Tell me exactly."

"All right." He snubbed his cigarette into an ashtray and kept grinding away at it even after it had completely ceased to burn. "I think we should kill Galina Rosmanov. Blunt enough for you?"

"Absolutely." She gave him a Viennese psychiatrist smile, the one that always accompanies a major breakthrough and signals the need for another score of sessions at a hundred bucks a pop. "I hope you understand why I forced you to verbalize it. I want it understood from the beginning that this is a joint venture. After it's over, we share the ramifications equally. We both lie awake nights wondering if we've done the right thing. We both break out in a cold sweat everytime a policeman glances at us sideways. We both bury our guilt under too many tranquilizers and deaden our minds with the silly chatter of vacuous people."

"I get the message. What say we store the lecture and move on to mechanics."

Michelle licked out the inside of her glass until it was as completely dry as the chalice after a final communion. "I've had my experts working on it ever since she came out. According to them, there's only one foolproof method." She pointed toward the private transportal winking at them through the open door on the other side of the room. "Essentially the same way we did it before. We drug her, stuff her into the wires, position her in a high-traffic strand where she'll be subjected to a great deal of electrical turmoil, and keep her there until she dissipates."

"If at first you don't succeed. You're sure it will work this go round?"

"As sure as I can be. Assuming no outside interference, the mathematics boys put the probability at eight-seven plus. The next best alternative, hiring a professional hit man, rates only a forty-three, and leaves a body to dispose of besides. I say we go with the numbers."

"How do we explain her disappearance?"

"We don't. She just one day drops out of sight. Given her reputation for outspoken dissidence, everyone will take it for granted that the Russians had her permanently censored. They will undoubtedly deny it, but nobody will believe them. We won't even get involved."

Michelle went to the wall, removed a picture and opened the safe behind it. From within she produced a vial of white powder, which she gave to Saul. "Odorless, tasteless, easily dissolved in any liquid, and guaranteed potent enough to keep even Wonder Woman asleep for six hours."

Saul slipped it into his pocket. His mission quite clear, he walked into the transportal room, keyed in the code number for his villa, punched the send button and disappeared.

CHAPTER 31

"You seem abnormally preoccupied this evening." Galina moved her dinner plate aside and folded her arms along the edge of the table. "Anything to do with my proposal?"

Saul experienced the tiny, near-subliminal pricks he had come to recognize as her attempts to pierce his mental blockade. "Quite frankly, yes. A few things about it still bother me." He unwrapped an after-dinner cigar and used the table's centerpiece candle to light it. "How long will it take? And what kind of state will I be in while it's happening?"

She folded her unsoiled napkin into a perfect square and set it beside her plate. For sheer tidiness, she put even Michelle to shame. "Your guess is as good as mine. I suspect at least an hour, and no more than three. As for your physical state, I would guess it will approximate a deep hypnotic trance."

"And once it's over, I will then possess all of your powers?"

It could have been his imagination, but it seemed to Saul that the pressure exerted on his mind intensified a notch or two. "Every single one."

Saul thought for a second and then said, "Let's get on with it, then."

She broke into a huge smile. "I assure you, you won't regret it."

Saul stood and went to the bar. "You mind if I have one last shot of courage?" He poured himself a stiff Bourbon and, for her, an orange juice. He raised his glass to shoulder level. "To us."

She took her glass and clinked it against his. "Soon to be unique in all the world." She swallowed the juice down.

She had barely set the glass aside when the drug began to have its effect. Her eyes glazed over. Her head would not stay upright.

She tried to stand, but her legs would not support her. "Saul, what have you done to me?" she wailed. "And why."

Saul tossed down another Bourbon anesthetic, but this one didn't ease his pain any better than the one that had gone before. "I think you've been playing me and a whole lot of other people for suckers. Rosie was the only person you didn't fool, maybe the only person you couldn't fool, but you solved that problem quite nicely by fixing it so that the two of you never made contact."

"Saul, what are you saying? I don't understand."

"I think you do. I think you understand only too well. For starters, I contend that you weren't as unhinged by Mary Hemke and her bullyboys as you pretended to be. I think you could have transported out of there anytime you wanted to, but instead chose to stick around and test out the destructive potential of your new powers. It was a perfect opportunity since you could always plead ignorance later."

Galina attempted to project herself out of the room to safety, but, unable to generate ample strength, succeeded only in blurring her edges. "I tell you now the same thing I told you then. I didn't realize I had such awful capacity. I didn't transport myself out of there because in my fright and confusion I simply forgot I could. It was still rather new to me, remember."

"But you certainly had the technique down pat when it came time to croak Felice Pierenska. Let me generate a scenario for that one. You transported yourself to her apartment, tortured her with strangulation, then forced her to take her fatal dive."

"You're crazy. I was here with you that evening. What evidence do you have that I wasn't?"

"Her neighbors heard a woman speaking to her in Russian."

"So what? Had I been there, I would have communicated with her telepathically. No one else would have heard me."

"Unless you became so incensed that you forgot yourself and started to verbalize. It has happened before. Besides, when the neighbors broke into her room, there was no one else there. You're the only one I know of who can make that quick an exit."

"Saul, Felice studied acting. She was quite capable of completely altering her voice. Perhaps her neighbors heard nothing more than Felice talking to herself." Galina intertwined her arms, as though embracing a ghost. "And what about my offer to share my powers with you? Would I do that if I were the kind of megalomaniac you seem to suspect me of having become?"

Saul ran his fingertips across the bartop, pausing at even the tiniest nicks and dings. "I don't believe you ever really intended to follow through. I think you only wanted me to drop my mental barrier so you could enter my mind and alter it somehow so I could never again resist your commands or block you out."

"That's ridiculous!" Her words staggered forth in a tipsy slur. "I had no such intention. Saul, you're not a vigilante. Don't act like one. If you doubt my innocence, then put me on trial. Let an impartial jury decide my fate. Decide it yourself, here, arbitrarily, and you instantly renounce every principle of justice you've ever stood for."

She was right, of course, and Saul knew it.

Unable to answer, he turned and walked out of the room. He went into his den, sat down at his desk, opened the top drawer, and removed a large sheaf of letters.

"Dear Mr. Lukas," began the one on top. "I don't know how I can ever repay you for getting me out of the wires the way you did." The letter had been written by the first traveler he had ever saved.

He crumpled it up and threw it into the wastebasket, then threw the others, thank-you letters also, in with it. There were so many they spilled over the top, and he had to mash them down with his foot to fit them all inside. Then he tossed a match in among them, and they shriveled away to a blackened jumble of meaningless words.

When he returned to the dining room, Galina was out cold.

Scooping her up in his arms, marveling for perhaps the last time at the supple musculature of her tiny body, he carried her to his transportal, activated it, and sent her to Bridge Authority Headquarters. He then stepped inside the transportal and went there too.

By the time he revived, Michelle had already completed most of the arrangements. Galina had been propped inside a transportal. A technician had cranked in a routing calibration which would feed her halfway through the New York City–Washington, D.C., strand, the system's heaviest-traveled line. She would be held there directly in the flow of traffic until she dissipated, probably within fourteen hours according to Bridge Authority mathematicians.

During the final adjustments, Saul grabbed a chair and dragged it as far from the goings-on as he could possibly get. But still he had only to look at the blank, solid walls around him and the stoutly locked doors to realize that, like it or not, he was very much a part of what was happening here. There was no way out.

Michelle gave him a status report. "Shouldn't be more than another ten minutes."

"Probably fly right by the way it always does when you're having fun." He leaned his chair against the wall, hooked his feet around the legs, and voiced his major concern. "You know, that's a fairly potent chunk of girl you're messing with. Are those theoreticians of yours positively sure she won't be able to harm the travelers who pass through her?"

Michelle dismissed his anxiety with a casual flutter of her hand. "That was one of our first considerations, and it came up negative. We anticipate no adverse effects whatsoever in that regard. She will pose no more of an obstacle to other travelers than would a random flux. Those who collide with her may be thrown slightly askew, but will be instantly realigned at the next collector station."

"You'd better be right on that one. I'd hate to see a monumental jam-up in there. Or worse. A whole string of freaks come pouring out."

"Absolutely impossible. We simulated it repeatedly on our big IBM and never got the slightest whiff of a problem. You just can't argue with those kinds of results."

The technician signaled that everything was ready.

Michelle nodded.

The technician punched the send button, and Galina was gone, replaced by an electronic blip on a specially rigged tracking map. Within seconds the map positioned her exactly midway between New York and Washington.

The emergency warning system flashed on as the malfunction indicators picked her up, but the technician in charge overrode, thereby automatically transmitting an *ignore* message to every other terminal directly linked to that route.

Then everyone sat back, poured coffee, and waited for Galina Rosmanov to disintegrate.

The first batch of travelers to hit her consisted of a group of nuns on a pilgrimage to Lourdes.

Next came a Little League team off to play in the Junior World Series.

Then a vacationing family of six.

Next a professional gambler on his way to Las Vegas.

Then a convicted killer bound for execution in a federal penitentiary.

Followed in rapid succession by nearly twenty-eight thousand others over a span of thirteen hours forty-seven minutes.

Until finally, the electronic blip that was Galina Rosmanov flickered and winked out of existence.

"I want to thank you," Michelle told the technical staff involved. "Come payday you'll find a nice bonus in your checks. As you know, this type of duty requires a mild memory wipe. So if you'll report to the dispensary, we'll administer the appropriate shots. They tell me it shouldn't delay you more than a few hours."

After they had gone, she turned to Saul. "No wipe for you, though. I want you to remember this forever. To know firsthand what it feels like to live with these awful decisions. To know you're not the pure, unsullied Resurrectionist anymore, the gallant crusader for human life and free will. You're one of us, now. A corporate hatchetman. Eliminating some so that the world as a whole will survive."

"Sure. Survive shaped in our image. The question remains, though. Is our image any better than Galina Rosmanov's?"

"I guess we'll never know, will we, Saul? I guess we'll never know."

CHAPTER 32

Later that day, Sister Maria Therese miraculously disappeared from her hotel room to reappear moments later in the front row of the Lourdes Cathedral.

Wendal Freitas scored the winning run for his Little League team when every opposing player who touched his blooper pop-up inexplicably dropped it like a hot potato.

Joe Garrett, fiftyish, pudgy, balding husband and father of four, committed adultery with no less than five women in a span of four hours. For some strange reason, none of these women could resist his advances.

Bob "Boston Beans" Hegarty won nearly half a million dollars in a poker game at the Sands. One of his opponents remarked to a bystander that it was like playing against someone who could read minds.

Gary Allen Nicholson escaped from his locked cell on death row leaving behind two guards both dead of strangulation.

And that was just the beginning.